Lost Cantos of the Ouroboros Caves

STORY RIVER BOOKS

PAT CONROY, EDITOR AT LARGE

LOST CANTOS
of the
OUROBOROS
CAVES

EXPANDED EDITION

MAGGIE SCHEIN

Illustrations by Jonathan Hannah
Foreword by Pat Conroy

The University of South Carolina Press

© 2015 Maggie Schein

Published by the University of South Carolina Press
Columbia, South Carolina 29208

www.sc.edu/uscpress

Manufactured in the United States of America

24 23 22 21 20 19 18 17 16 15
10 9 8 7 6 5 4 3 2 1

Library of Congress Cataloging-in-Publication Data
Schein, Maggie.
[Short stories. Selections]
Lost Cantos of the Ourobouros Caves :
expanded edition / Maggie Schein ; illustrations
by Jonathan Hannah ; foreword by Pat Conroy.
pages cm. — (Story River Books)
ISBN 978-1-61117-471-7 (hardback) —
ISBN 978-1-61117-472-4 (paperback) —
ISBN 978-1-61117-473-1
(ebook) 1. Fables, American. I. Title.
PS3619.C3464A6 2014
813'.6—dc23

This book was printed on recycled paper with
30 percent postconsumer waste content.

CONTENTS

FOREWORD

I met Maggie Schein on the day of her birth. I was present in the waiting room as her mother Martha went into labor with her klutzy, unhelpful father, Bernie, in feckless attendance. Bernie and I had become best friends in Beaufort High School and that friendship continues until this day. One of the luckiest things about that connection is I got to watch Maggie grow up in all her eccentric magic.

Maggie never dressed like other little girls—I was raising three of them down the street, myself. Though she always dressed herself with style and attitude, it was a difficult ensemble to classify. She dressed in materials that looked like they were gathered from dempster-dumpsters located outside of gypsy camps or a wardrobe that fell off a train carrying a traveling circus. There was always a brazenness and comedy in her approach to the world—although I would've strangled her with great cheer when, at age eight, she put her new tarantula on my head and let it walk along the center of my face, pausing only to fiddle with my nose hairs. Though she had a dog and a few cats, Maggie's heart belonged to her tarantula.

From an early age, Maggie Schein was precocious in strange ways that portended a wild-eyed curiosity and an easy association with genius. But it was not language that held her full attention: She first fell in love with the grace, and the cunning, and the suppleness of the dance. For twelve years she gave up her life for ballet, that stern apprenticeship. I saw a dozen of her dance performances with a pre-professional company in Atlanta, but missed her during the New York years. She made her body lithe and hard as she joined the Feld Ballet/NY and then Hartford Ballet. The phrase "corps de ballet" has always served as one of the most beautiful groupings of words, and Maggie was on her way up when she sustained a career-ending injury, which also just happened to coincide with a deepening bent in her mind for studying philosophy.

Like all ex-ballerinas, the future became a curious-yet-terrifying opportunity for her. She knew she didn't wish to participate in that fate of most ballerinas—opening up a small studio with pretty boys and girls struggling at the barre, illuminated by great mirrors that could reflect the present, but had no idea about what the future may hold. And so she dove into the world of academia first at New York University and, then at the University of Chicago's famous Committee on Social Thought, where, when I asked if she missed dancing, she said she "learned how thoughts have a music, a rhythm of their own and words can be aligned together and articulated to create the shapes that move to those rhythms, so in some way," she told me, "I am still dancing." She studied with the esteemed South African writer, J.M. Coetzee, who would later win the Nobel Prize. It was there, in Chicago, that she met, conferenced with, and partied with some of the great minds of our times.

After writing her dissertation on naturalistic ethics and receiving her Ph.D., Maggie found herself washed up on the shore with word fragments all around her in tide pools and sand drifts and nautilus shells. She found words calling to her from the air and from the sea and she made two fists of sand on the beach, and cascades of words fell beside her. Maggie was taken prisoner. The language had seized and held her in a grip that would not loosen. Maggie came to me when she had something to show that she'd written. You trust the guys and the girls who are there when you are born.

First of all, I found myself dazzled by the utter, plainsong beauty of her prose. I've always been one of those readers ensnared by the bright flow of language and the masters who can hurl that language into the air to make new galaxies for a tired-out sky. Instantly, I knew I'd discovered a grandmaster with Maggie and her book flew me out toward the great books where ideas were as original as the words themselves.

Once in Rome, I met the great Italian fabulist, Italo Calvino, at a coffee bar after I had recently finished his book, *Invisible Cities*. My first impulse was to drop to my knees and kiss his ring, but he seemed much too shy to endure such an outrageous gesture. I've mentioned my admiration of Calvino to all of my friends and many have fallen in love with his work, but many also despise him. Because Calvino writes with such breathtaking subtlety, he's not understood by the literalists of this world.

Robert Jordan and I both graduated from the Citadel and I never realized the enormous power of his series of books called "The Wheel of Time" until after his death. A friend recommended—no, she forced upon me—the works of George R.R. Martin, and these writers set up in my cotillion bells of memory my first glorious encounters with Stephen King, Edgar Allan Poe, Anne Rice, and the great Tolkien himself. When I open a book, I command that the writer turns me inside out, earns my respect with ideas and encounters I've never dreamed of or imagined in my most crestfallen nightmares.

In 1982, when I was living in Rome, the novelist Jonathan Carroll sent me his first novel. It was called the *Land of Laughs* and I was enjoying it with pleasure when two dogs began talking to each other. That stopped me in mid-sentence, but the book had already grabbed me by the collar, I finished it and called Jonathan right away to tell him how much I loved his novel. Now, I've been reading Jonathan Carroll for thirty years and his work is strange, hallucinatory, and necessary. He opened my mind to fictional worlds I had never traversed and my life's been richer for it. Recently, he sent me a copy of his collected short stories and there's the sweetness of magic on every page.

Though Maggie Schein calls her stories "fables" I'm not convinced that's an accurate title. But because Maggie went to the University of Chicago and I went to the Citadel, she is a lot smarter than I am and wins every argument with me.

Maggie Schein has written an oddball, perverse work of genius. Her fables are a genuine seeker's attempts to bring order to the world, to subdue chaos, to establish laws among tribes that are brand new to language. Omens abound and eagles scream truths from a thousand feet and every line is a poem that brings order to a restless universe. She writes a sentence like a string of black pearls and I believe a cult is about to form to track her future path as an artist. She won't give you a single thing of what you want, but she'll give you a lot more. Her Cantos seem enchanted to me, as if they were some secret language found on the rear ceilings or the walls of Lascaux. Her realm is timeless and enchanted and braided together with all the power and seduction of myth herself.

Maggie Schein writes like a fallen angel, and I was there on the night of her birth.

Pat Conroy

THE SERPENT
AND THE
BOY

The great peak of the mountain was visible from nearly anywhere in the small village. From the well, it appeared to be an ordinary mountain peak. From the butcher's shop, however, as from the home of a young boy with soft green eyes, it appeared to be an arc, like the crest of a wave forever suspended. From the exact center of town, to those who stood and watched with dutiful silence and attention as the sun passed directly over it at midday, it appeared to undulate subtly, like the chest of one who is content. When a storm approached from the west of the mountains, one could hear a faint whine, as if the wind had to pass through something unexpected. To the snake, who often sunned herself under the boulder at the edge of the forest, each crevice and ridge in the mountain was a perfect match to the contours of her body. She did not wonder about the true shape of the mountain's peak, since she already knew it.

The village inhabitants who were old enough to remember the day the butcher returned from his trek up the mountain often dropped their eyes to the dusty ground when it was in view, as if its image were a reminder of humility and of the danger of trying to be too great or go too far.

To most of the youths in the village, the great mountain was merely the backdrop for legends from long ago that one outgrew rather quickly—no matter how the old men and women swayed when they told of them. Such ecstasy eluded the youth and made them itch beneath their skins. The young had many pleasures to seek and many things to accomplish so that they could become strong, beautiful and savvy. So, lonely stories of the crazy butcher, or the hunter before him, or the mad witch who was said to have given birth at the very top to a baby she buried alive in a silver lined box, were of little interest to them. For them, the well would always be full, the butcher would always be crazy, and the elders would always tell nostalgic stories about fantastical people whom they felt no need to try to understand.

The old man who lived at the outskirts of town, however, remembered quite vividly the day the butcher returned. When he was a young boy, his father had told him of the hunter who disappeared into the mountains during his lifetime, and of the mad witch who was said to have given birth at the peak hundreds of years ago. He often thought of these stories with passion: for those who conquered the mountains, who passed through the impassable, despite whatever flaws they had, tried to be great. To him, the pleasure of learning—the aspiration for greatness—was clear. He could not understand why the young resisted it so. "So much so that they refuse to learn and see!" he thought to himself.

As he sat on his porch, he raised his chin and thought about how much he enjoyed the short-lived moment of new knowledge: that moment wherein one can see where one was from where one is, and the ache of change transforms into a pleasurable rumination about how the new accords with the old. One can tinker a bit with oneself then, before time continues on its way. "It is," he thought, "really the sense of power over oneself that is so compelling; of being both the clay, the pot and—in that moment of reflection—also the potter." He could teach the young such delights, he thought, if only they were interested.

The old man had done many things in his time: he had desired so badly it nearly destroyed him, been so satisfied that he nearly forgot to continue living, chased what he could not have, acquired more than he dreamed he would, walked through ancient towns with sand blown buildings and seen the pyramids up close. So he was content enough, now, to sit and rock. The only thing he had left to do was to pass on to those who came next what he had learned. That, he thought with satisfaction, was perhaps the most precious lesson he had learned in his long life. The old man enjoyed that his blessing was to have come far enough to help others on their ways. He eagerly anticipated the visits of the one young boy with the soft green eyes, who often came, asking the old man to teach him what he knew.

"It is too bad," thought the snake, who often watched the old man from a nest of leaves at the base of her sunning stone, "that he takes pleasure in that which he does not truly understand."

For the snake understood why the young resist change—despite often being hungry for power and success. Real change does not leave one the luxury of contemplating it or the illusion that one gains mastery from it. She coiled herself tightly, enjoying the scrape of the leaves against her belly, and she concentrated on soaking up the heat from the earth, trying to ignore the satisfied thunk and whistle of the old man's thoughts.

The old man turned his head towards the line of trees, looking to see what had made the dry leaves rustle. When he saw nothing, he rocked in his chair and allowed himself to return to worrying about how to tell the village youth of what he knew.

It was not the snake's habit to concern herself with other people's troubles, but from her post under the leaves by the large rock at the edge of the tree line, she had been unable to avoid taking in a certain series of events. Doing nothing about them, which was her habit, had become oddly oppressive to her. And being oppressed was far more troubling than acting out of the ordinary.

"I really haven't the patience for this," she thought. "There is a reason snakes do not get involved in the troubles of others." But this old man, and the boy who came to him seeking his wisdom, they were treading awfully near to her turf—and even if it is not a snake's duty to help one in distress, it is certainly permissible for her to honor her turf.

Just as she felt her tail end glide over a particularly moist bit of decaying leaves, she heard the eager steps of the boy running towards the old man's front porch. The boy's mother, who was wiser than her appearance revealed, had warned him on his way out that day that he did not know the depths of his own desire, and that he should watch where he stepped. But he went anyway, not knowing what she meant. He ran through the town, slowing only in front of the seamstress's shop, where the girl with the large sad eyes often sat, looking towards the center of town. She wore very pretty ribbons in her hair, he thought.

"Old man!" he said, trying to catch his breath as he approached the porch. "Yes, boy?" "I know what I want, now. I thought and thought, just like you told me to, and I know what I want to do!"

The old man was relieved at that moment but the deep lines of his weathered face would not let his enthusiasm show through—for he did not want the boy to know how eager he was to teach a child who truly wanted to learn. "And what, boy," he said calmly, "is it that you discovered?"

The boy pointed over the trees, to the highest peak of the great Ouroboros mountain. The old man guessed it was probably one of the biggest mountains on the continent, but he couldn't be certain of that. He knew that in his lifetime alone a few had aspired to reach its summit, but even fewer had returned, each seeming oddly broken to him. So it must be a big mountain, indeed. He remembered the dawn that brought the ragged butcher back into town. The butcher, rather than being reborn from his journey and framed by the delicate morning sun, stumbled and wandered as if the dawn had found him unpalatable and spit him out. Even now, his knife, though it made clean enough cuts of fine meat, seemed to fall with an unexplained heaviness as if it would never actually cut through what was before it—his store, however, received plenty of business, being in the center of town and such.

"Yes, boy," he said. "I see the mountains. What about them?"

The boy put his finger down by his side and said, very solemnly, "I want to climb over them. Can you teach me to do that?"

The snake, having suspected this was coming, released herself from her coil and launched herself to the deepest part of the forest under a covering of leaves, where the old man's thoughts should not be able to disturb her and she could think clearly.

The old man stopped rocking, knowing that his moment of truth had arrived. He looked at the young boy, nearly a young man—with bones too long for his muscles and a mind that had determined to master a soul that was not, just yet, convinced of the mind's authority.

And the old man, who could usually feel the layers of the breeze against his skin like different sheets of fine fabric, and who could usually see individual blades of grass with the crisp precision of one who thinks himself satisfied and free, began to grow a bit disoriented. He did not know, at that moment, from which direction the wind blew, and the stretch of grass between his porch and the tree line seemed an indefinite expanse of green. He was sure that the project of showing the young man how to train, how to overcome himself, and how to climb a great mountain was a worthy outlet for all of his learning. So why, he wondered, did he feel worried instead of relieved?

The boy saw the old man grip the arms of his rocking chair, and he noticed, for the first time, how smooth the wood was—"weathered," he thought, "but unworried—just what one could want in a wise man." He smiled slightly, as he realized that he had chosen well. "Here is a man who can take me where I want to go, and not only that; no, much more than that! Here is a man who seems to want to!"

He waited for the old man's reaction, and he worried only slightly, that what he had chosen was not a worthy task. But he had thought, and thought about it during the preceding days, and he was quite confident that conquering the mountain, stepping all the steps that it would take to reach the other side, these were not petty endeavors. He wondered, what he would feel like when he saw the other side? How much more capable he would feel? How proud of himself? He shook his head slightly . . . No, that was not it . . . how much he would be able to trust himself. That was it. That, he thought, if the old man asks, is what I want from this. To see from whence I came, and to trust myself. And I will return home a man, and I will be proud to present myself to my family and to the neighbors! Maybe I will even know what to say to the sad young woman at the seamstress' shop to make her happy.

But the old man did not ask what the boy wanted from his journey. The boy had chosen a task that would test his discipline, his intelligence, his wisdom, and his physical and mental strength, thought the old man. The task would teach him that he can go beyond his limits, that he is bigger now than he thinks. If he were successful, it would teach him that he can trust himself, but more than that—the old man relaxed again and let his cheek fall into the eastbound breeze—when he reaches the other side, he will look back and know that he is not who he was, and he will share with me the pleasures of true learning, the gritty pleasure of knowing that one can overcome oneself. And this, thought the old man, palming the smooth arms of his rocker, is what I want.

The snake, having traveled deep into the forest, had, until now, been blessedly free of the old man's precious thoughts. But, just at the moment the old man thought his last thought, she snagged her underbelly on a sharp branch. She stopped, flicked the air with her tongue, and immediately tasted the sourness of sentiments overripe with delusion. "Cursed old man," she thought. "It is one thing to think wrong thoughts, it is another to think wrong thoughts that will affect the life of a boy who seeks true knowledge." She remained there for a moment, still flicking her tongue rapidly against the distasteful air. What the old man wanted, she thought, was company. He wanted to make a man of the boy, a man who was indebted to him, with whom he could share the breeze, the blades of grass, and the other subtleties of life. She unhooked herself from the branch that had snagged her and rubbed the descaled segment of her belly in some soft dirt. She continued on, now knowing that she must do what she had hoped she could avoid. "It is not an easy lesson that I have to teach," she thought. But the reader should not be too sympathetic: snakes do not take to sympathy, and besides, she was designed to teach her lesson, as were all snakes who came before her and who will come after her.

When she arrived at the center of the forest, she stopped. Though there was no prey in range, she raised her neck, as if to survey the area. She swayed gently back and forth until all the serpents who had been and who will be raised their heads and swayed with her. In a rare flash of introspection, she said outloud, "We are so misunderstood." For one brief flick of the tongue, she indulged in the thought that after all this time, people still believed that her ancestor had offered sin, had offered knowledge of good and evil—what a tragic misunderstanding! That, she thought, is not what a snake knows—we do not distinguish good and evil—and thus, no serpent, not even the infamous one in the famous garden, could have tempted Eve with such a promise. The people were right though, she permitted herself to continue, that what she offered was a sort of death—a cycle of mortality—but oh the distance from this fact to the interpretations of it that had overcome the world! The snake snapped her head this way and that, trying to shake off the dramatic thought that it was not, by the way, her nature to have. But we should excuse her slip of character: for at the moments when one is called, finally, to perform the tasks for which one was created, it is easy to slide into uncharacteristic indulgences.

The old man, having recovered his sense of the world, turned to the boy and said, "Yes, boy. I will train you. We will begin in three days."

The boy, having read enough parables in his time, neither argued, nor asked why. Rather, he nodded, smiled to himself, and turned toward home, though he was eager to begin his journey right at that moment.

After three days, the boy returned to the old man's house. On the way, right in the middle of the dirt path, he saw a large snake, laced with the most brilliant earth tones. He saw that the snake was beginning to molt, bits of clear scales freeing themselves from the pure muscle, so he knew that she would not attack. He continued on and reached the old man's house to begin his long journey.

The old man trained the boy day in and day out. Often, in the evenings, they could see a large snake paislied with green, black and browns—very much like the one the boy had seen in his path on that first day—circle the yard. One evening, while the boy and the old man were taking in the light of the sunset, the boy saw the snake slither up the near side of the porch. The boy stepped back, startled. But the old man said, "Boy, digest your fear as the snake digests the rabbit. Do not let it out. Do not be afraid, for snakes feed on fear, and therefore, only attack when one is afraid."

For one brief moment, the snake wished she had eyes mobile enough to roll. But, as they were fixed and black, she had to be satisfied with flicking her forked tongue viciously at the old man—as if to say, "You fool! We are here precisely to warn you to be afraid! You should be afraid! You do not know of what you seek!"

But the boy did as he was told, and gulped down his fear whole—which, he thought, felt far larger than a mere rabbit.

The snake laid her head down and propelled herself down the side of the porch, eager for the serene stillness of the earth again.

The old man took pause though and thought that perhaps the snake's appearance was something to be considered. But he was not sure what to consider. Perhaps it was enough, he consoled himself, to teach the boy to swallow his fear.

The next evening, the snake was nowhere to be seen, but a perfect snake skin, with translucent greens, blacks and browns, lay like a flag on the front steps of the porch.

The boy and the old man continued to train. But the snake did not appear again.

When the boy was so ragged with exhaustion that his spirit began to shine, just a bit through his tired muscles and worn out mind the old man knew that he was ready.

The boy, hardly able to eat or stand, smiled to himself and knew that in a short time, he would stand at the peak of the Ouroboros Mountains, and finally rest. Oh, such rest had never seemed so sweetly deserved. He would stand there, arms raised, and know how far he had come. And the old man thought, "Soon, I will have a companion. A young man who knows the individual blades of grass, who, with his confirmation of the beauty of the world, will make me young again!"

The old man walked with the boy through the village, where he said goodbye to his family, and through to the far corner of the forest to the base of the massive mountain. He told him to stay there for the night, eat his fill, rest, and at the crack of dawn, begin his journey. "I will see you when you are a new man," he said, and hugged the boy.

The boy watched the old man leave, and he did as he was told. He ate his sandwiches, put his pack under his head, and then closed his eyes. He woke, however, far before dawn, startled by something rustling in the leaves. When he sat up to look, he saw the starlight glance off an enormous green snake, muscles contracting and expanding as if she could take in and digest the mountain itself. He remembered what the old man had said, and concentrated on the snake, watching her until his fear took on the rhythm of her movements and was no longer his own.

He woke again at dawn and began up the first rocky slope. Many days passed, and he walked each one, guided by the still and peaceful peak of the mountain, which he could see now was not one peak, but two arcs, reaching towards one another and joining just at the top. At night, when he could walk no more, he dreamt of lying between the two ajoined arcs, deserving of the cradle their base would make for him.

On the seventh day, he looked up and realized that he could no longer see the peak of the mountain. He began, for the first time, to worry a bit that he had not kept a straight course. If he had not, he could be wasting precious time and energy. Or worse—he felt panic cinch his stomach—he could be circling, nowhere near the peak, destined to round the mountain forever and never reach the top! Oh! He bent over in exhaustion and a sudden nausea. But what, he wondered, had he done wrong? He had listened to the old man; he had trained; he had studied the mountain! He had watched for the peaks!

Just then, out of the corner of his eye, he saw the beautiful green snake curled up and soaking in the last bit of heat from the fading sun. He was not afraid. He was too tired and angry to be afraid. The snake slowly unfurled herself and slithered down the rock. She headed directly for the boy. She hated to do this, but one must do what one must. She slithered around his heels, and just as he looked back, she sprung forward and as gently as she could, pierced the skin on his ankle. She extracted her fangs before too much venom had been released—it was always tricky, gauging how much would be enough, but not too much. But experience had served her well. The boy gasped and began to feel the venom rise in his veins. He grew dizzy, hot, and thirsty—so thirsty, but he could not make his hand reach for his canteen. He fell to the ground and lay there. He was aware that he was not dead, but he was not sure he was alive either. He was unable to close his eyes, which is what he wanted to do more than anything.

The snake slid by his head and around to the front, where he could see her. She raised herself, and she said to him: "If you want to reach your goal, you will follow me. I will show you how to get there, but you must know that the path you have chosen is very difficult, indeed, and what is more, you must be willing to shed who you are to become what you want to be." The boy knew this. "Why," he thought, "was the snake telling him this? Of course one must shed the old to become the new!"

"That, my friend," said the snake, who seemed almost golden now in the glow of the sun heavy with its own brightness, "is not what I mean. You have already shed the fears you began with, as well as the weaknesses, and you will reach your goal, but you cannot have it once you are there. This is my lesson. Contemplate my words. You have this whole journey to do so. When you understand what they mean, only then can you reach your goal and have it."

But then, the snake thought to herself but did not say aloud, you will no longer need to have it.

When the next dawn came, the boy woke, picked the leaves from his hair, rubbed his sore ankle, and felt terribly disoriented. He took a drink from his canteen and looked for the touching arch of the peak, but he still could not see it. The snake, having taken in the clean heat of the birthing sun, was refreshed and eased herself into view—not so quickly as to startle the boy, nor so slowly as to be ignored. When she knew he could see her back glinting in the sun, she licked the air and began to move. The boy not knowing what else to do, followed the path of her confident, rhythmic sway through the leaves.

He kept his eye on her for what felt like days. At last, she stopped. He looked up and gasped at the great peak. So near! What a perfect circle, with a perfect cradle! And I will rest there! And then, thought the boy, inhaling the pure air, I will walk with purpose down the mountain. And I will walk again into the village, and I will stand in front of the old man, and I will . . .

But before he completed his thought, he found that he was already standing in the circle formed by the two arched peaks. And there, he saw, was no cradle—merely a ledge barely large enough for two adolescent feet. The snake was winding her way up one of the arches to a place where they joined. The boy steadied himself against the other arch.

When she reached the top, she dropped her head down, just before his face. She swayed there. He watched her.

She said to the boy, "Can you hear me, or must I bite you again?"

The boy, though dizzy, could hear her. And he thought of his still smarting ankle, so, he nodded and looked, for the first time directly at the snake.

She continued, "You have reached the summit, my boy. You have shed your fear and your weakness, and you have trained hard and sincerely. Look now. Can you see the way down the mountain?"

The boy looked to where the down slope should be: where the victory walk, the one he had so anticipated, would take him . . . but he could see nothing, as the sun was descending again, and had bloomed completely in the circle created by the two peaks. He felt himself growing dizzier as he realized that there was no other side of the mountain. There was no way down.

"No?" the snake asked, "you cannot?"

The boy had to admit that he could not.

"Good!" said the snake. "That is good! There is only one way down for one who climbs sincerely. And for that, my young brave man, you will have to follow me closely. Or," she said, "You may turn around and go back the way you came, undoing the steps you worked so hard for."

"And do not suppress your fear. What we are going to embark on is great enough to deserve your honest fear."

With that, the snake lifted her head away from his, gripped the upper part of the circle with her tail, and, it seemed to the boy, propelled herself straight into the dense light of the sun.

So the boy reached his arms out, stood on his tiptoes, and leaned forward. He fell, but not fast at first: for he felt the heat catch him. "The weight," he thought slowly, "who knew that the heat of the sun had weight enough to catch one's fall!" But then, as he cleared the circle, he began to fall more and more quickly, and he could see the snake above him, twisting and gliding through the air. He felt the breeze created by the fall of his body cradle and release him, moment by moment as if he were a leaf; and then he felt the particles of water in the air, denser than those of pure breath, tickle the hairs on his shoulders and neck, and he felt the last tentacles of the sun rush through his veins like blood.

As the sun collapsed itself into darkness, the boy did not see the ground approaching, nor an ocean. He saw, rather, the old man rocking on his porch, and he saw how lonely he was. The boy saw that despite all that the old man had accomplished, he had never learned that the accumulation of years would not fill his soul.

He saw his mother, and how, though she bent humbly to gather the clothes from the wash basket or pull water from the well, her spirit was busy laughing at the extraordinary cleverness of the wind and the absurd peace and vigor of the earthworms. He saw that when she was alone, she smiled to herself, knowing that the breath of her spirit guided her.

He saw each of the people he had ever encountered—he saw the butcher and knew that he kept a secret turned inwards that bloomed like a mushroom cloud inside him, preventing him from making his way out; and he saw the seamstress, who gathered herself together like a spider taking back its web because she would not live to see the coming fall.

He saw the beautiful young girl with the sad eyes and the ribbons in her hair. Her belly was full with a child who, though a cause of shame and confusion to the young girl, would be the fulfillment of another's prophesy. And he saw that though some of their lives had been painful, and some would become painful, while others would be free, or full of pleasure, each had a net carefully woven for it by its soul, so that its spirit would not stray too far.

Finally, he saw a young boy, eager to grow into what he would become, eager to manifest the magic in his bones. The boy was long, and his muscles had not yet grown to accommodate his length, and he, he saw, with tears in his eyes, that the boy wanted more than anything, to become what he was to be.

And here I am, breathed in the young man who used to be the boy, but the air was so rich, so full that he could hardly hold it in his lungs.

Many weeks had passed since the boy had begun his trek to the mountain. The old man waited and waited. He rocked on his front porch and he worried the smooth arms of his chair. The boy's mother, at first saddened by the disappearance of her son, could still smell his breath on the breeze when she was alone, and so she knew that he was well. The butcher, one day, ran from the town before he had finished carving even one serving of meat and was never seen again. A newborn was found near the well, and though the girl with sad eyes grew sadder, no one knew to whom the baby belonged.

The boy's body was never found. But on the other side of the mountains, in a town that also had mothers, and butchers, young beautiful sad women and old men who yearned for company, a stranger appeared one day. He seemed confused, but not distraught about his confusion. He wandered the town, not quite knowing what he was looking for, but sure that someone there could show him. He wanted, he thought, to make manifest this magic he felt coursing through his bones. He wandered and wandered, until finally, he came upon an old man who rocked slowly in his chair—eyes nearly shut and his face turned towards the sun. The young man approached the chair, but the older one did not turn: he just smiled into the sun, which seemed, at that moment, to cup his face, as a mother's hands cups the face of her child. The young man stood back. When the old man finally turned to him and opened his eyes, he said to the newcomer, "There is something I want to learn. Can you teach me?"

THE
QUESTIONER

Even the most ordinary patterns of life and thought—those we most take for granted—must be carefully checked and mended lest they fall apart from wear or age. In fact, it should be no surprise that the Ordinary is especially vulnerable, since it is the most weathered. The seamstress, who checks the seams and reinforces them and patches the worn spots, is usually content enough with her life and the majority of her work. She hums a familiar tune while she pushes the needle through the fabric of What-Everyone-Knew-Would-Happen, and around the edges of That-Which-Would-Follow, and reinforces the seams of That-Which-We-Find-We-Had-Already-Known. She has been over these many times, but that is okay. In fact, she finds comfort in the repetition. She knows that the places most likely to wear are the ones people run over and over without ever looking and the places snagged by the terrific grief of people tripping over What-Happens-to-Everyone, and the explosive joy when they round the corner of Fear. But she knows, also, that the shape of the fabric will change. And she hides her anticipation behind the tune she hums day in and day out.

After too much repair, the most ordinary spots become thick and inflexible. They become bewilderingly difficult to navigate. What used to be pliant suddenly rejects the weight of a person's most sincere intent. What used to be invisible becomes a mountain beyond which one cannot see. And then, the threads begin to rebel. The seamstress waits for the moment when her familiar tune suddenly stops and the needle will not push through the fabric. Each day, she wonders, if today will be the day. And it is okay that nearly all days are not the day. For the day eventually comes.

The day was nearing, for it was an oddly precarious time in the seamstress's village; the people had mastered much and were, for the most part, content. The water in their well was kept pure by a filter designed by the engineer. The children lived through the many complications of childhood, thanks to the wise and to the doctors. The old suffered less. What had been discovered by those before had been meticulously recorded by those who observe. The children were taught what was known to be true and then went on to teach others as they had been taught.

The seamstress felt the fabric of the ordinary toughen. She smiled in delight, therefore, when her habitual humming was finally interrupted by a stubborn silver thread that refused to submit and would not find its place in the design.

She fingered the silver thread and tipped her chin to the sky. The thread was wiry, bright, and downright defiant. It would need a whole new pattern! She pulled it out and laid it aside. She ran her hand along the embroidery of the stars, and she felt the rift where That-Which-Was-Not-Yet would have to be sewn.

When the people become content, it is time for new questions to enter the world. Those who bear them are gilded with a certain brightness to compensate for their odd role, for the world will not conform to the contours of their spirits the way it does for others. In fact, it must not, or else they will never break through. This is why they must wait until the Ordinary has become dense and rigid.

So the seamstress carefully took the thread and began to embroider a robe specially made for the boy who, she knew, would eventually find his way to her door to ask her questions that only he could answer. Since she could not offer answers, at least she could offer him a picture of the sky as it was when he was born.

When the boy was an infant he could command the world. If he smiled, so did everyone else. If he cried, the windows opened and fire burst forth from the stove, and feet pattered this way and that, and then the world became tight and warm and satisfying. When he waved his hands, larger hands fluttered gently to meet his like down feathers. With his every move, the shape of the world changed, as if he were the axis. When he learned to crawl, each shuffle forward revealed a new landscape —one smelled of the kitchen, and one of burnt wood and one of musty wood and one of his parents. In each one, he finally learned to stand, and still, the world leaned into him and waved back, and made it clear that his mere thoughts would create the universe.

At the park, the dogs padded up to greet him, sniffing, wagging, and touching their wet noses to his neck. The geese tottered behind him and pecked at his diapers. The gulls did not scatter when he walked through them, and the spiders momentarily paused their weaving—as if to say, "See, this is how it is done"—when he stood marveling at them.

But then, as happens to most of us, he learned to speak. In the beginning, he found that speaking had much the same effect as smiling or crying or waving his hands. But the more complex his speech grew, the more confused he became about its effects. He spoke and nothing much happened—or rather, what happened is that the world around him seemed to get farther and farther away from him.

Like a good boy, he had learned to put his words in front of his actions. He had learned to say what he wanted before simply grabbing for it. When he passed the peacock who patrolled the town's well, he said, "Mama, I want to pet the bird!" But instead of feeling the tilt of the bird's pleasure against his hand he felt his mother's hand firmly push his own back to his side. "The bird is not yours," she said. And the boy felt, for the very first time, alone.

When he went to school, the square walls and measured steps of the teacher reassured him. Here, he thought, the world will come close enough for me to touch it and break it open. In his classes, he spoke and spoke, but nothing happened. The world did not change shapes. The chalk succumbed to the blackboard; the teacher scratched her pencil against paper. The glue in the book binding crackled as students searched for secrets that only adults seemed to value. Each day he went to school; and each day, it was the same.

When the teacher's attention was trapped between the board on which she wrote and the notes in her hand, when each child in the class read as if the words on the page might make him good, the boy felt the whole world to be unbearably still and so terribly far away, as if it too were afraid. He thought, at first, that perhaps the world was just sleeping and that is why it would not respond to him. His father, he knew, sometimes slept very, very hard. One had to jump right on his chest to get him to giggle and to make his arms arc up around and hold one in. So the boy climbed up on his chair, and he yelled at the top of his lungs as though hurling a large rock into a perfectly still pond. He stood tall, and smiled, waiting for the world to ripple and return his greeting.

The corners of his smile were brought down bewilderingly as his arms were pressed to his sides, and he was carried, like an unwieldy box, to the headmaster's office. The world had not woken up. Rather, it had turned its back and huddled away. It asked him to step quietly. To not try to get its attention. It told him to compress. To keep his hands inside. He was too loud. He was too big. He was too much, it said. The stillness of a classroom cannot be made to smile back at a little boy. But why not? he thought.

And so went the boy's first experiences of rejection. Which is why, when he was older, he did not even blush when the girls turned from him whispering and giggling. He never sought friends or a wife.

For many years, he kept his hands busy and safe, fingering the seams of his pockets, tracing the threads over and over. He spoke only of what had already been talked about or asked. He smiled when smiled at. One afternoon, he ventured to extend himself when the girl with the sad eyes wore new purple ribbons in her hair: He told her they were very nice ribbons—but only because as she fingered them during class, she created a vacuum between herself and him that drew his words out. And he did think they were pretty ribbons. But that is as far as he thought. Any further and he might again let himself out only to be stuffed back in like a jack-in-the-box that wasn't supposed to spring. So he turned away from her. He found the answer in the book to the question the teacher had asked.

He offered the answer. It was taken as water flows downward.

Why, he wondered, was it so important that he find an answer that everyone already seemed to know? For there are so many questions, he thought! If we each spend all of our time learning what has already been learned before, then we will never get anywhere!

The more he answered the questions asked of him, the more he did as he was told, the more it seemed to him that the world was sealing itself off from him. The wind skirted him, the squirrels scattered when he came near, the spider slid to the most hidden corner of her web when he stood in awe at its construction. He ran to the field and he waved his arms and he smiled, but even the leaves seemed to ignore him.

He was not happy. Water flows downward, but he wanted to make it splash and to see the universe reflected in the droplets that splashed up and out, he wanted to hear its chaotic laughter as his body interrupted its prescribed path.

Those of whom one might ask genuine questions about the world—teachers, parents, and priests—looked down and smiled at this jittery child, with hands that leapt about and fluttered like a pair of fledgling gulls. When he asked them how to make the wind circle in his hand like a whisper, or how to see the universe in a droplet of water, or where to dream so that he could see himself before he was born, or why he could not talk to the soul that lived in his goat, they undid their smiles and said, "My boy, first you must learn the simple things: Like why the sky is blue and why a straw looks bent in a glass half-full of water. You must know that tomatoes are fruits and that there have always been wise men, though no one we know has ever known them. There is much to do; the world is full of interesting questions to which we have found the answers. Why don't you run along and play with those?"

The boy tried. He ran diligently from each question to its answer in this or that book. But the distance was so very short, and the path so worn that it had lost all resilience. He returned from each journey, grasping the answer he had plucked from one book or another, but found that he had nothing to give anyone that they did not already know.

"Do you know," he would begin telling his father, trying to muster some excitement, "that female spiders live longer than males?!"

"Yes, child. Is that what they taught you in school today? That is very good." And then he returned to his work and told the boy to go on. The boy did not feel it was very good at all. In fact, by this time, the boy had grown very sad that no one cared that they could not herd the threads of the wind, or that the rain fell indiscriminately, or that they did not know who they had been before they were born, or when the anniversary of their last death was.

So, on his way home from school one fall afternoon, he took a detour by the prairie where the deer often grazed in small groups. They fascinated him; for not only were they extraordinarily poised, but also so conflicted (and this, we know, is a compelling concoction for any boy)—the calm eyes and deliberately delicate steps in such tension with the quivering ears and the tail alert in the wind for a change that would indicate a predator.

On this afternoon, he stepped quietly towards them. The doe nearest him blinked her elegant lashes and lifted her nose. He raised one foot and set it down one step closer to her—so slowly that he could feel the grass bend beneath his foot. The doe subtly shifted her weight onto her rear legs, flicked her ears, and watched the boy without looking at him. The wind volleyed between the boy and doe, telling the doe with crystal precision how far the boy was from her, though she could not tell from his scent if he meant her harm or not. Finally, the boy could hold off the chase no longer: He saw her flinch ever so slightly and he punched his foot into the grass and rushed her. She cut, darted, and he followed. The others stood still for a split second, before they too began to carve the field with their zigzags and leaps. He ran after one and then another, and when he was in the center of where they had been, he stopped and looked around. His doe was still in sight, and she too stopped—dead still as if he were no longer there. So the boy leaned forward a bit, as if to prod her with his mere thought. Just as he was rounding the arc of his anticipation, waiting for her to turn and bound through the woods, he heard a whisper from the edge of the tall grasses that surrounded the field.

"Stay still," the voice hushed. "Do not move towards her. Do not move away from her. Do not look at her." The doe stood as still as the boy. "Slowly lower yourself to the ground."

The voice was so fine, so intense—so nearly inaudible that the boy was not sure he heard it at all. But he did as he was told.

Once he was sitting, still as he could be in the grass, the tiny world of buzzing and climbing arose before him—the brown cricket paused on a wide leaf and looked at him askance, as if to silently indicate that perhaps the boy had misplaced himself. The sweat bees hung low and swayed towards the boy's salty knees. They swerved slowly and drunkenly so that one might think they meant no harm. The black beetles kept the pace they had always kept and maneuvered around the boy as they had always maneuvered around obstacles for thousands of years. The hornets dove in with preemptive threats. The bumblebee pretended he did not notice the boy and busied himself with the clover, modestly hoping not to be crushed if a chase were to give way.

The boy was so dazzled by the array of movement and sound, that he did not hear the crisp grass part as the grey wolf moved towards him. The wolf silently lowered himself down beside the boy.

The boy gasped. The wolf raised his blue eyes against their black rims towards the boy and said, "Shh! Lay your head next to mine so that I do not have to raise my voice."

The boy looked at the majestic head and the shocking eyes and, again, he did as he was told—for wolves do not ask. He could feel the warm moist breath, and he could see a faint clear gloss on the black nose—which despite the stillness of the rest of his body, seemed to strain and twitch in all directions at once.

"My boy," whispered the wolf, "you are confused. What are you doing out here, chasing the doe and the herd? You are not a wolf." He sniffed at the boy's hands, as if to make sure. "You are not a lion or even a coyote."

"No," agreed the boy sheepishly. "I was merely trying to make the world move. It is so still, rigid, and so worn, and no one seems to notice! But the doe," he hesitated while he searched for the right words, "she moved for me. And I felt as though in the chase, something new opened up—it was like we were dancing!"

The wolf blinked and sniffed the air.

The seamstress fingered the rift in the seams of the sky again, hoping to feel an edge of what was to come. And she was rather elated that she felt nothing but an electric void.

"What would you have done," continued the wolf, "if you had caught that doe? A tango? Perhaps a jig?"

"I would have petted her. I would've soaked in the sublime brown of her eyes, and I would have asked her to play more games with me."

The wolf snorted gently and flicked his right ear, which, the boy noticed just then, looked incredibly soft. The wolf raised his head, the deep of his eyes fixing on something the boy could not see.

He turned back to the boy and he said, "Child, this is not a game to the deer. It is not play to her. When you chase, she does not experience an exchange between her and the world. She sees the near end of her world."

With that, he rose with the exact sway of the grass. He opened his jaws just slightly and inhaled the midline current of air so that it grazed his palate with a map of where each deer was holding stillness around her. He blinked once, and then he tore through the grasses faster than the boy's eyes could follow. When the boy finally saw him again, he was standing over the doe, his ribs heaving in and out. He picked her up by the neck, which was wet with sweat and blood, and dragged her over to the boy. The boy turned away, embarrassed by the awkward, silly clack of the doe's front hooves against one another.

"This," the wolf said, nuzzling the doe's warm head, "is why they run. Look into her eyes now."

The boy could not, and the wolf, thinking his point harsh enough, did not force him.

"They do not run because you chase them. They do not run to help you shape the world into something that fits you. They run because if they do not, they never will again."

The wolf looked down at the doe, who lay with one eye to the sky, her neck bulging in an unnatural curve and her tongue hanging uncomfortably between her teeth. "It has nothing at all to do with you," the wolf looked to the boy and said.

The boy stood silent, looking neither at the wolf nor the doe. He could not swallow the saliva in his mouth. He was too stunned to even cry, but the tears boiled in him until they forced themselves from him in heaves—not only because the beautiful doe was dead but because he had been so terribly wrong. He felt his soul collapse in on itself and he wished he could hide it away—but a soul is far too large to hide.

After the wolf had taken the doe to his den, he returned and asked the boy to walk with him. "You think," he said, his ribcage swaying between his front and rear legs with an odd vulnerability, "that I am cruel? That my lesson for you was cruel?"

The boy did think so, so he nodded. And he felt terrible that the doe was a sacrifice for his lesson.

The seamstress retrieved her hand from the sky and returned to mending the ordinary as best she could: For before the boy had created a new pattern, the rest of the world still had to walk the old one.

"But then you have missed the point again, child. Run your hand along my back."

The boy did and felt, under the coarse grey hair, thick bones and muscles coiled with experience.

"Feel along my jaw." The wolf stood still so that the boy could run his hands along the softly sculpted muscles. The wolf swiped his tongue along his nose and said, "If you bare your teeth, what are you saying?"

The boy wasn't sure, so he curled back his lips and squinted his eyes—but he felt foolish rather than fierce.

"Exactly," said the wolf. "We are made for different things, just as the doe is made for different things. It is not a dishonor for a doe to die in the jaws of a wolf—a coyote maybe—but not a wolf. I honored the fright and the chase you carelessly ignited in her with what it is intended for. In this way, I restored to harmony what your game disrupted. If there was cruelty there, then you were the cause and I, the remedy.

"But do not be too hard on yourself—your mistake was an easy one to make and your drive is earnest. You cannot make a new space in the world by ripping through a harmony that is already there. You must find the openings that are made for your hands. When you do, the seams will part effortlessly.

"Walk with me, and I will take you to the seamstress. Perhaps she can help you see that yours is not to break what little is beautiful, but to unveil a beauty hitherto unseen."

"The seamstress?" the boy asked. Why, he wondered, would a wolf know a seamstress, much less believe that a mere costume-maker could help him!

"You have seen the strength of my legs and my jaws," the wolf said, as if hearing the boy's thoughts. "You have seen the truth of harmony; the complementary exchange in the world can appear harsh—and I, as the bearer of it, can appear cruel. But look closer, child. I have not always been what I am."

The boy looked, and all of a sudden, the rounded ears appeared larger, and the stern intensity of the wolf's face appeared soft and pleading. The pads of his paws too large for lithe maneuvering. He saw a creature whose face pleaded for shelter and protection and for a split second, the boy wanted to hold him.

"Ah!" said the wolf, "so you see? I was once very young. I did not know how to kill or that I was supposed to want to. My brothers and sisters, they knew way before I did, and so my mother picked me up in her mouth and carried me to the seamstress. She wove for me . . ." the wolf trailed off, allowing himself a rare moment of nostalgia, "She wove for me many furs." He finished and smiled, keeping his sharp canines hidden beneath his memories. "Some of us come with some of our seams a bit undone, or with a skin that doesn't seem to fit quite right. In such cases, it is best to see the seamstress."

When they arrived, the seamstress was busy at a machine, her foot pumping rhythmically and her hands following one another in a never-ending loop. The boy tried to catch a glimpse of what she might be sewing, but try though he might, he saw nothing. There was no fabric, no thread, only the whir of the long needle pumping up and down, the gentle clank of the pedal and the seamstress's face tipped upward smiling at the music of her work. He noticed that she did not seem to be watching what she was doing, and he tried not to flinch at the thought of the great needle piercing her fingers.

The wolf swayed his head and drew from the center of his soul the sweetest, softest howl. The seamstress's foot halted midstroke and she raised her hands slightly and inhaled, as if to take in the sound with her whole being. She smiled, as if the howl contained thoughts so well shared between her and the wolf that they needed no explanations.

"Well, hello, my great grey wolf!" she said—without looking at him.

The wolf lowered his head and said, "Hello."

"I see," said the seamstress, "that you have grown into yourself quite handsomely."

"I have become what I am," said the wolf, "no small debt to you."

The seamstress felt her way along the sewing table with her hands and said, "I see you have brought me someone in need of mending?"

"Yes," said the wolf.

"Oh, I see!" said the seamstress, reaching a hand out to touch the wolf's head—though she did not turn to look at him and the boy wondered if she saw anything at all.

"Well, my boy," she said turning to face the boy, "tell me your trouble as simply as you can."

The boy thought. He thought about what his teachers had said; he thought about how much his heart ached—first with joy and then with pain—for the doe, and, as he was a very genuine boy, he said, "When I wave and smile at the world, nothing waves back. People only want me to learn what is already known and my footsteps echo so loudly it is as if there is no one else in the world. The world does not see me."

"Yes," nodded the seamstress, gently. "Yes, that has been true." And the words were so light and clear that they sliced right through the boy, releasing a spout of tears from him.

She offered the boy a handkerchief and said, "But this is not a matter of mending that which is torn. What needs to be woven has already been designed. You are merely wearing yourself inside out. You think the world does not see you, but that is because you have been facing the wrong direction."

The boy understood from her tone that she believed what she said made absolute sense, but he was not at all sure, in practice, what she meant. He thought to himself, "I have been facing the wrong direction. So, how do I turn around?"

He shuffled his feet on the wooden floor until he was facing the other direction, towards the doorway. He looked to the left and the right. Nothing much changed.

The seamstress laughed and the wolf softened his face in kindness—for real wolves do not laugh in the presence of young boys.

"Yes!" chuckled the seamstress. "That is right! Face the other direction! Look out the door! Walk into the world!" She clapped her long calloused hands, which made the boy all the more confused, since upon following her directions, still nothing at all seemed to change.

Draping the boy in the robe she had made from his silver thread so many years ago, she said, "When you feel lost, wear this. I could not sew you a new fur as I did for our wolf, or weave into the world an opening for you, but you do not need that. So I made you a robe that will remind you that you were not born to receive from the world what it already has. You were born to create the answers you seek." Down the front of the robe was a most intricate silver web that curved all the way around the hem to the underside. The boy followed it and saw that on the inside the whole galaxy was embroidered, with the constellation of Cygnus in the thick silver thread.

"But I do not even remember my questions anymore!" the boy pleaded.

"Mmm," grumbled the wolf and he lay down in the doorway, "they will catch you. Just keep walking and they will catch you."

"And what am I to do now?" asked the boy, fingering the silk robe, and feeling more lost than ever.

"Walk with me back to the field," said the wolf.

So the boy walked with the wolf, and the wolf said to him along the way, "You, like I, cannot help but be what you are. Every now and then, when no one is looking, put on your robe and remember that though we can not show you where to go, because we have not yet been there, that is what makes your particular journey all the more worthwhile."

So the boy went on. And the wolf was right: The questions returned, lightly at first, and then in swarms that caught the boy's mind in their dazzling rush.

In school, while the teacher reminded the students to check their answers against the back of the book, he wondered about where his soul went to find dreams. Why, on some nights, did it present him with landscapes of mountains, burnt orange sand, and exotic creatures, and on other nights, the sad girl from school—who had now become a melancholic young woman—who liked to put ribbons in her hair? How, he wondered, could he see girls turn into dragons at night, and see only the cardinals calling to one another during the day?

While his family talked during dinner of the neighbors and of work, he smiled to himself and wondered with such sincerity where all the wizards were that the wizards themselves heard his wonder and sent a flash of lightning across the unclouded sky to tease him. Certainly there must be wizards, he thought—for there are so many stories about them.

In this way, many years passed. The boy became a young man, and though he no longer fought his questions, he had not found any answers. One summer afternoon as he was passing by the well, he remembered what the seamstress had said—that he was facing the wrong direction. He stood still, and then he turned in a full circle. He looked up, and saw the same sky that he knew was blue because, as the books had said, the atmosphere scatters the blue light waves, which get caught in air.

And then he heard an odd sound below him: a faint gurgle and rustle. He expected to see the old peacock, but when he looked down he was stunned to see, lying quietly by the well's stone wall, an infant girl with a silk ribbon around her head. He looked about, for surely her parents must be near? But he saw no one. So he leaned forward, peering at her, pausing before he acknowledged that everything was about to change. And when he saw that her eyes began to widen, taking in the largeness of the world, he could not help himself and he took his blue robe from his shoulders and he wrapped her in it and picked her up. He held her away from himself at first and wondered what in the world is a young man to do with an infant girl? He wandered around town with her, asking if anyone knew of her parents. No one seemed to know what to do with her. Everyone had somewhere they had to be, or children of their own to attend to, or lovers to pursue, or books to read. The closer he held her to him, the more tiny he realized she was.

When the girl began to cry, he didn't know quite what to do and so took one of her naive hands and opened the palm. He whispered into it over and over that she need not worry, that he would take care of her, and the wind, drawn by the velocity of his feeling, whirled around his words in her palm. The girl's eyes crinkled and she smiled, feeling the wind weave between the young man's quiet words and tickle her palm. She giggled and took his large hand and turned it over and over, as if there she might discover the most fascinating things. And he giggled in agreement and smiled at how simple it was to make the wind swirl in a hand like a whisper!

When evening fell, and still no one claimed the girl, he took her with him to the field, and he lay on the grass under the stars. The crickets were busy serenading the dew, and the dew gently vibrated in resonance. The beetles and hornets were burrowed away for the night. So he laid the child on his chest. He took her hand again and said, "Look right up there, into the sky. I will show you how I was born." He took her tiny fingers, which were just the right size for grasping the smallest stars, and he moved first Spica, Hydra, and then with his own hands, he nudged Saturn, Mars and Venus into position. When he was done, he checked the sky against the underside of his robe and gently clapped the girl's hands together, for it was perfect.

"Now," he said, "let us see how you were born!" He closed his eyes and wrapped his hands around hers, and as she was falling asleep, he followed her out and together they moved first the sun, and then the moon, and then arranged Ursa Major just so, and Draco, and when the sky was just right—she was more sure than he of the right placement, for it had not been so long that her soul had forgotten—he slipped into the spaces between the darkness, and found himself inside a drop of dew in which he could see the whole universe pulse in rhythm with the cricket's dutiful sounds.

The seamstress woke early the next morning, eager to weave the first threads of the new into the old.

THE PRIEST
AND THE
SWAN

It was an old village. It was protected by a mountain with a mysterious peak that was host to legends of witches, young men, old men, and serpents from whom the mountain was born. The mountain sheltered the well, the square and the fields in which the lives of the inhabitants played out. History in this village had been lost, and found and refined a bit, and so now, the people knew that—whatever else they didn't know—they wanted to be loved and they wanted to learn to love. And this, this makes them like most other peoples, in most other villages, really.

What some of the villagers did not yet understand was that there are different kinds of love: The love each one has to offer and the love his or her beloved needs may be very different, and this can make love complicated.

The Monk, in whose soft green eyes the grass saw itself reflected—who, legend has it, simply arose from the base of the mountain one day as a young man, as though born from the mountain herself—spent his days by the pond in the field where the river went to rest. He came to keep silent solidarity with the Swan, who circled the pond, stroking the water with her feathers as a mother does a sleeping child. She was not supposed

29

to be there, the Swan, and the Monk loved her for it—for she was a glitch in the order of the ordinary: a glitch not made by the sharp obstacles people so often throw in their own ways; nor by blind desperation, which can pierce through the fine filaments of the order; she was, rather, a glitch by choice, by tenderness, through which the divine leaked in. Her heart had snagged on a sadness of the world, and she had decided it best not to leave it.

The Swan could have gone on; she could have flown away, she could have taken her place as one of the austerely beautiful in the world, or one of the esoteric and mysterious—those being the two, rather royal, positions Swans may hold. But she did not. She circled her pond, creating soothing ripples, protecting and keeping company a group of souls under her who would never even know she was there.

What the Swan understood, which many of the villagers did not yet, was that to love is to cherish; to cherish is to provide, at the most critical moments, the deepest of the beloved's needs. To be loved is to have that which one needs in one's most critical moments.

There are, she knew, very different sorts of "critical moments," and thus, there are different kinds of love—some of which may be so lonely that they do not feel like love at all. The Swan took on this last sort for herself.

Her defiant effort endeared the Monk, tendering his heart with a mixture of sadness and joy.

At a certain time, along the coast of every ocean, the souls of the newly dead huddle at the edge of the water's white foam like sea turtle hatchlings. As the tide comes in, they are, as the poets say, taken out into the deep, where they will each deposit into the ocean the sediments of life on the land, and where they will soak in the ocean's great blue.

How then, certain souls came to this pond, to be unknowingly caressed by the strokes of this Swan, who was quite indifferent to the affections of this Monk, is a long story.

On one warm and rainy afternoon, the Monk's reverie was interrupted by the erratic footfalls of a breathless young boy, playing chase with a dragonfly. The boy and the dragonfly stopped for a moment when they came to the pond so that the boy could catch his breath, and the dragonfly hovered over the water, mesmerized by the syncopated shadows of his wings. Down below the water, strange shapes shied away from the reflection, and the Swan calmly swam between the dragonfly and the water to shield them from it.

As the boy waited for his lungs to settle, the rain began to fall in slow heavy drops that slapped the boy's forehead playfully and clung to his nose before they fell away.

He turned to the Monk then, who seemed to be smiling though his lips were not curved. "How is it," the little boy asked the Monk, "that one can love God so much that the rain feels like tiny joyful fingers all over your face, but that still one can never know Him?"

"Well," said the Monk, who often said the strangest things, "maybe it is because God's love is less like rain, and more like snow."

The boy wondered over these words in the fresh days of winter, when the leaves opened themselves, eager for rain, and died, slowly under the weight and cold of the snow.

From the first frost of late November he went to the pond and he watched the snow turn to droplets and drip from the Swan's soft back. He watched the pond-water take away the edges of the flakes, as though welcoming them home. During the days of December in which the sun grows weary, however, he saw the waters change just a bit at a time: first around the edges and then in little spots in the middle—it was so gradual that the water, he imagined, did not even know she was being turned to ice until it was too late and the last ounce was pinched silent in mid-ripple.

During the winter, the Swan nested at the bank of the pond until it was frozen solid—she left then only because those beneath it would be kept company by their reflections in the ice, like children too young to recognize themselves in a mirror.

The young boy watched the bright petals of the mums in the field present themselves to the sky—their doubtless faith that it would nourish them evidenced by their crimson upturned bowls. He watched as they held themselves open, despite the fatal accumulation of luminous white flakes. He watched them cradle the snow, as if embracing anyway that which refused to nourish them.

"This," he wondered, "is love? What a cruel trick that the petals are shaped perfectly to absorb enough frost to wilt them by morning and kill them by nightfall!"

He was disappointed in the flowers—or in the rain for disguising itself as snow. He believed that love should, as depicted by the frescoes and stained glass through which the sun lit the churches, carry one across the great threshold from burden to light. And so, out of his own desperate need to believe that the crimson vessels were created for their preservation and not for their destruction, he decided to become a priest.

On the day of his ordainment, he made his commitment to God that he would learn all he could of love.

And he was not surprised—though he was saddened—when, in his adult years, he sat in the father's quarters of the confessionals and heard his parishioners describe love as though it had fallen on them like snow, when they had opened themselves to receive rain.

And when the woman with the auburn hair and the purple ribbons came to pray, and then to sit on the other side of the latticed window to confess, he reminded himself that his personal satisfaction of love was not what he had promised to either God or himself.

He watched the light between the dark wooden lattice play on her brown skirt. The wind, neither kindly nor maliciously, brought to his nose the smell of the herbed oils she had rubbed through her hair. And he gently disregarded his nose. He saw her fingers running over one another like a dragonfly's wings. So he gently dismissed his eyes and his hands. He could feel how her heart opened to joy, as the mum's petals did in the field, and he quietly told his own to beat to its own rhythm, lest it fall on hers now as snow. Finally, then, he heard her confession.

"Bless me, father, for I have sinned," she began. And he reminded himself, silently, that it was not he who blessed her, but God. It was God's love she was after. And he gently disregarded himself. He offered her the blessing, prescribed a slight penance, and reminded her that through her effort and her love of Christ, Christ would take on her sins and redeem her before God. The Priest dutifully listened to the rest of the confessors while he waited for the next Sunday when the woman with the ribbons would return.

At her wedding, he officiated and saw the way her husband's shoulders fell towards hers in angles of affection and charm. He saw how the husband's mouth moved, stopping only when it received a smile or a laugh from her. He saw the way the air between them sputtered, leapt, and played. He was glad it was not he who had to love only one woman. For his commitment was to love all who came to him and he felt relieved that he was not burdened by the thick business of love between one person and another.

Not many years later, the husband—his eyes and hands heavy with grief—came to the priest and said, "My wife is dying." The Priest went to her bedside in her last hours. He felt that he knew her well, and that she knew she was forgiven, that she had loved well and was well loved, so she could go peacefully. He was shocked, therefore, when she grasped his robes and pulled him to her, and said, "You must help me! I do not want to suffer in purgatory! I do not want to linger among the living as a shadow that can neither see nor touch! I am afraid," she said. "I am afraid of getting lost in the quiet and in the cold!"

The Priest was shocked by the ugliness of such pure fear. He took hold of the thin hand it had stiffened. "Child, if you have confessed your sins, you are safe from hell and from torment. You have given your sins to Christ and you have bound your soul to a man as in the image of God and he has vowed to protect you beyond death. I was there at your wedding; he made that vow before God in my presence. I do not doubt his faith to either God or you. It is dishonorable for you to do so."

"Every time she wakes up," said the husband from his chair in the corner of the room, "she moans about the dark and the cold. She says there is no sky, no earth, no air, no forwards or back and she will get lost."

The woman's grip became fiercer and she opened her eyes so wide—as if to force the Priest to open his mind—"Yes, I married a good husband and he has loved me with a pure heart . . . But he cannot see me in the dark and so he will not know my soul there."

"What does this mean, he does not know your soul?" asked the Priest. "Did I not join his to yours in marriage?"

The woman closed her eyes, her attention drawn to the fly buzzing at the window. She smiled painfully. "He knows," she said, "the smell of sandalwood in my hair; he knows the way my hands scurry when I am nervous, he knows how to make me laugh and he knows how to make my laughter feed his own. He loves me . . . and he will not know how to let me go—he can already hear the absence of my laughter and he can already smell the house when only he is in it and he cannot see in the dark. I am too young." She opened her golden eyes and looked at the Priest.

"Did you not want him to see your beauty as a reflection of your heart? Did you not oil your hair so that he would delight in its scent? Did you not want him to take the flutter from your hands? To hold you when you were afraid? There is no sin in this!"

"Yes," she admitted, and turned her head away for a moment, "of course I did. Of course I did. But . . . he loves me too much. He has not yet learned to see me through white hair, the arid smell of old skin, to see my heart through eyes watery and blue with age. He has not yet learned who I am when there is nothing left to say or do . . . He cannot stand when I am in pain and he must look away—and this is because he *loves* me. And now, I will have to go alone, and at the moment I need him to see the most, he will have to avert his eyes," she said, desperate to make herself clear.

The Priest looked at her auburn hair, and the tired beauty in her eyes. He watched her mouth and wondered what it must have been like to have been loved by such a woman, a woman who knew what her husband saw of her, who knew the holes in life that she filled for him and who knew how to make openings in which his heart could echo.

"He promised to love you for eternity. And I will give you the nourishment you need for your journey to eternity: trust the love of God through men, child, your husband will find you in heaven when it is his time."

But at that moment, the Priest was shaken. He had the strange sensation that he, in fact, did not know the root of her fear and that, as a man concerned with the way love moved souls, he should be. Here she was, attended to by two men who loved her deeply, how could she worry? And the beautiful dying woman, who had come so faithfully every Sunday to offer all she had—minor sins of the mind, of habit, and of a pure heart— did the unthinkable:

"Devil, who knows his way in the dark, take me, instead!" she cried to the ceiling with her last breath.

The Priest crossed her quickly, began and finished the viaticum, and closed her eyes—hoping that her journey would not be marred by her last words. He did not feel the peace he usually felt at death. Rather, he felt the vibration of the fly's resilient body against the windowpane as its uncertainty about why it did not, with all its persistence, make it to the tree in the yard escalated. He felt the weaving of the dust under the bed. He felt the tug of the woman's hands on his cloak, though her fingers had retracted their hold on life.

The black moth, who had been quietly waiting in the corner of the room, rushed to the ceiling light as though he had forgotten something, singeing each of his dusty wings relentlessly.

As the souls relinquish their sediment and absorb the blue of the sea, they begin to travel with the currents. Some reach the surface and are greedily swept up by the clouds only to fall again in a well, or on the forehead of a child playing chase with a dragonfly in a field. Some are heavy and run fast with the undercurrent to tributaries in far reaches of the world. Some stay in the ocean for a very long time, riding wherever it takes them, mesmerized by the rhythmic peace of the jellyfish, the frenetic angles cut by schools of silverfish, and by the oddly striking resemblance between an owl and an octopus. But for some, the movement of the ocean does not offer calm: For they cannot shake the fear of their journeys.

The Priest wondered why he felt such dis-ease, but he made himself return to the church, take his position in the confessional, listen, prescribe, and assure—as was his duty. Most of the parishioners did not trouble him: They had the sins that people are destined to have. They suffered for them and tried to learn to honor Christ by giving him their suffering. And with his calmest tone, the Priest whispered to the children of the church, "Show your devotion to Christ, our father, by honoring that his currency in heaven is worth more than all the tears you could ever cry. He can redeem more than you can sin and He can suffer for it with more purity, and through Him, you will cleanse your own soul."

Until the woman's husband came for his confession, the Priest had believed that he had been fulfilling his role of lightening his parishioners' hearts through their confessions. When the husband came, he did not sit down on the oiled bench; he did not ask for forgiveness, nor cross himself. He grabbed hold of the lattice and yelled through it: "I failed her! She died with such fear, and pain! And I could not protect her from that. Was my love not enough? How did I fail her?" The Priest was silent.

At that moment, he was struck breathless as the image of the crimson petals straining to open themselves against the snow broke into his mind; he saw the hearts of his confessors as the mums in winter, and his words collecting in the warmth of their trust like the snow—and his knees painfully hit the oiled oak floor. "I have," he thought, "been telling them that their own hearts are not enough to do what they were born to do . . . not enough to direct them to good, not enough to repent, not enough to cleanse their own souls, not red enough to melt the snow. Mine is the voice that tells the petals to remain open for the rain, despite the frost. But that is because," he admitted, "it seems true: even the love bound by God through the sacrament of marriage is not enough—not enough to keep the moth from the light, and not enough to nourish the hearts of the confessors."

He could see, around the frescoes of Moses and Jesus and the Mary in Mourning, bewilderment whispering about. He saw the black moth, calm on the porcelain hand of Magdalene.

The moment of truth eventually comes for all of the dead. The waves toss them and turn them like shells, smoothing away the mundane of the life that was. When the moon stops pulling so hard on the tide, and before the morning winds stir the water, the ocean settles down. The shells hang in the deep like ornaments, twisting this way and that and taking in their true weights, their colors, and their shapes.

After the sea has tumbled them, some are left very very small, having not accumulated much of substance in their lives. Others are ornate or large, having collected enduring essence. The light ones are carried quickly by the waves back out to another shore, for they have much to do before they can house a creature of the sea. The heavy ones sink to the bottom. Some rest there for a while. Some are inhabited by creatures who carry them on their backs to specific shores. Some ride the biggest waves in, eager to display their sculpted shells to the outer world.

For others, however, the memory of the journey to the ocean overwhelms them—they do not see the sand as massaging away the nubs and scars; they remember only the tumult and confusion as the first wave hit them, the nausea of the ever-spiraling line of the horizon.

The Priest sat in the pews all night. He watched the descent of the sun transform Mary from young and bright to somber and pensive. He watched God's fingers darken and grow distant from the stained glass garden; in the darkness, the whites of Moses' eyes became lit by the moon; Gabriel's white robes and Raphael's golden staff glowed. The Priest wondered how he could be surrounded by so many angels but be spoken to by none of them? He was trying so hard, and surely he needed their help!

When morning came and the light from God's fingers again lit the great tree and the serpent, the Priest rose, but his ribs pressed against his lungs and he could hardly catch enough air to walk. He would not hear confessions today, for he had one of his own to make.

He walked out of the church, and towards the fountain that was in the center of the square. He watched the people walk around him, turning or bowing their heads, avoiding or confessing silently as they passed him.

He watched as a young boy ran from one vendor to another, feeling a purple silk scarf at one and running his fingers along the hilt of an unsharpened sword at another. And he watched the old man, who everyone said was crazy, shuffle around the fountain as he always had—though on that day, he seemed to smile a bit. The Priest wondered what the old man could possibly have to smile about, and why that sparrow perched on the fountain seemed to watch him as though he might become a tasty morsel at any second.

What makes the fearful and timid souls most fearful and timid is not that they did not get what they wanted from life; it is not, as many believe, that they were not loved or did not love. There are other ways to be damned than this. The ones who genuinely did not give or receive love are not beset by fear, but rather, by determination—they return as the mesmerizingly lovely, the sincere, and the noble with eyes that compel even their enemies to smile on occasion. No, the timid souls, who were calmed by the gentle paddling of the Swan, were afraid because though they had believed that they had gotten what they wanted from life, they were surprised, at the moment of death, to find that they had not. And then, of course, there is nothing left to do about it, and there is nowhere to turn.

The Priest wandered past the square and to the quiet field. There, the sun had reached the point in the sky where it could see nearly everything, and everything stilled itself, submitting to the daily inspection—except, of course, the Swan, who continued to paddle gently around the pond—for the sun does not reach those for whom she was paddling.

The Monk sat motionless, watching the perfect ripples in the water, until the silence was interrupted by the deliberately cautious footfalls of the Priest.

"Welcome, Father," said the Monk and patted the grass beside him for the Priest to sit down. "What is on your mind, my friend?"

The Priest sat by him for a moment before speaking. "Brother," said the Priest, "do you know why the angels don't speak to us anymore?"

"Perhaps," said the Monk, "It is simply that they have nothing left to say. They have been speaking of love for so long now, and not much really seems to change. Perhaps they have given us what they can and told us as much as they know. Perhaps they do not know as much as we would like them to."

The Priest shook his head. "Then it is we who are failing? We are not learning how to love?" He thought of all the humbled spirits that came to hear of Christ's love on Sundays. So many people mean to love! And they mean to love so much! How could nothing have changed? How could love fail to grow? But, of course, people also came to him, in all phases of life, because they felt that they had tried so hard to love, and yet many of them too felt that love, despite their efforts, had eluded them or had eluded the ones for whom their love was meant. The woman with the auburn hair, for instance, and now her husband. And the Priest, like the angels, had nothing left to tell them.

"And you?" asked the Monk gently. "Has it come through you as you expected?"

The Priest stayed silent, for they both knew he would not be sitting there if the answer were yes.

"Let me tell you a simple story, then" said the Monk, the soft green of his eyes accented with sharp flecks of gold. "What does a child need from her father?"

"Love," said the Priest.

"Of course. Attention, affection, joy. Play. Yes. Of course. That is what love feels like to a child. They lick it from the smile-creased eyes like honeysuckle dew. A parent's greatest pleasure is seeing the child drunk on that dew, no?"

"Of course!" said the Priest. "Surely that is love in one of its purest forms."

"Surely it must be," the Monk agreed and began his story: "Now, there is a child whose curls seem to cradle happiness. One afternoon, while she is out with her father, she discovers that she can climb the great pine tree near the edge of the forest. She sees something unusual, something shiny way up in the branches. She climbs so very, very high and gets a good grip with one of her hands on one of the long branches. As she swings, many, many feet above the ground, she calls to her father, 'look, Daddy! Look at me!' The father turns his face to the tree, smiles, laughs and tells her she is like a monkey; he dances below her making 'Ooht,

ooht' sounds, while he lifts his feet in a silly way that makes her nose crunch up with glee and her heart swell to her fingertips—for it is the blessed fate of children that their bodies are small enough that their hearts can reach to fill every part of them—the white angels clap, for this is human love, surely, if any is.

"So the angels watch the father, and the father dances for the girl and, meanwhile, the tree worries. Though she can hold great weight, she cannot change what will be, and she cannot shrink her trunk which has become too thick for the little girl's fingers; nor can she smooth her bark that has begun to grate against the girl's tender palms, which slip and twist as she swings. The tree cannot move the safety crook of her trunk nearer to the girl's foot, which keeps just missing it. And the father does not see. He does not see the girl lose her grip, and once her grip is lost, he cannot catch her. And so she falls, and eventually, she dies of her injuries.

"For years the father stoops beneath a viscous layer of shame, believing not just that he failed to love her enough—for that, one would hate oneself. No, he believes he loved her as best as he could, with all his might and that his love was not enough.

"He goes to the church to confess, but what is he to confess? What is his sin? The angels gather around him, silently, for they do not know what to tell him. Their job was to remind the people of love, and this man loved with all his might. And so they turned away and fluttered against the stained glass windows like a hundred moths.

"Your woman with the silk ribbons and the auburn hair," the Monk said to the Priest, "she was like that child."

The Swan glided around the blackened pond, feeling the water push against her slick feet and trail in perfect arcs behind her. She was so gentle, as if she were stroking the backs of children, lulling them to sleep for as long as they needed in order to forget that they were afraid.

"What, father, is it that you tell your parishioners that we live for?"

"To enter the gates of heaven and live eternal life with God."

"And what carries us across the golden bridge, to reach the gates?"

"Love carries us."

"But?" said the Monk.

"But it seems that some souls are too heavy . . ." said the Priest quietly.

"Take off your robes. Fold them. And, if the Swan permits us to enter the pond, then we will see a love story that is very different from the ones you know."

The Priest slid off his robes and folded them, tying his golden cord in a figure eight. The Monk kneeled at the edge of the pond and beckoned to the Swan. She came, though her head arced away.

"Please," he said, "it is so he can see—so that he can understand that love is never less than enough; it is that human beings just do not know which kinds of love to use for what and for whom."

"No," said the Swan, lengthening her great neck towards him in sympathy. "I am sorry, I cannot. Some need to remember, and some to forget, and it is the latter who concern me. It is the former who concern you. We each know our place. That is rare enough: Let us not disrupt it."

The strange shapes in the waters floated peacefully under her, smiling and frowning—as those with Alzheimer's do—because it is their habit. With each of their dips and dives, they shed the reasons why.

"Walk to the cliff to where the river begins to dip underground," the Swan instructed them. "Cast your net, and you will see clearly enough why they come here, and why it is so important that they forget their fear. There you will see the need for the hardest kind of love for a human being to imagine."

The Priest and the Monk walked to the hollow in the cliff, where the river slid underground. The Monk put his heart in his hands and dipped it into the water. The earnest red pulsing was bait enough to draw a thin soul which circled it in wakes of panic.

And of course, since nothing is random in the universe—except by men's feeble calculations—the soul they caught with the Monk's heart was, indeed, the soul of the young woman with auburn hair.

"What has happened, child?" asked the Monk.

"I don't know," said the soul. "The man I loved could not see in the dark and I was alone. And the water was so cold and the waves tumbled so fast that I could not tell where the horizon was. I called and called for someone to help me, for someone to tell me it was okay, but no one was there. When I saw his reflection in the abalone, he was drowning in his own salty tears, telling me it would be okay, but he was so unsure—you see, even he was afraid for me. His love made him afraid for me. And so there was no one to tell me it would be okay, or where to go, or how to breathe underwater, and so I died, again and again. Until I could die no more. Now I am headed to where the river ends. I hear it is peaceful and one does not have to die there, again.

"If I do not make it to where the river hides from the ocean—if you or something else stops me and I must go back—then I assure you that I will return stripped of all kindness, all beauty, and all love. I will be a thorn with no flower."

The Priest caught his breath and said, "Why, child? Why would you forsake the love of God through men? Were you not loved?"

"Because I need someone whom I can trust to see in the darkness. And that trust must be bigger than my fear; someone who does not tend to my fear. The 'golden bridge' is not lit with stars, and it is not accompanied by the singing of angels. If anyone stays with me through the tossing of the waves, pointing to the line of the horizon so that I do not become nauseous and ingest that which I have expelled, if anyone's voice tells me it will be alright, then it will be only because they know the way, and because it must be done. They will tend to me because I have lived and learned and because I am a soul—not because of what I am leaving behind."

"Go rest, child," the Monk said. "Follow the water under the earth and to the pond and swim there knowing that you will be safe and that you are guarded by an undying faith." With that, he released her back into the water and the men returned to the pond.

The Priest watched the Swan, now. She swam to them and spoke, for the second and last time.

"I swim here because the ripples keep the souls from remembering their lives, and therefore, their deaths. And though we would all like to remember . . . some need, most of all, to forget before they go on again.

"It is not, as the cynics believe, that there isn't enough love in the world. Rather it's that people find themselves in the wrong positions— those that need love in life become bound to one another by death, and those that need love in death are bound to one another by life—and this prevents each from giving what he can and receiving what he needs. And so each goes away believing that the love they were born to understand will not touch them."

The Priest could not help but hear in his head the vows that indiscriminately joined people in life and death . . . with no thought to the sort of love their souls needed or of what they were capable of giving. He thought of all of those he had counseled to love their enemies . . . when perhaps their enemies were merely trying to ensure a guide in the dark.

"It is an unfortunate fact of life," continued the Swan, "that the deepest needs of some do not coincide with what one would like to give them. One would like to nourish their lives. One would like to give them joy. One would like to give them inspiration and desire. For these are the things of life, and life is wonderful. But there are some for whom tenderness towards life makes death more painful.

"For the more tender and innocent the life, the more dying is a matter of trust—trust that the other is strong enough to withstand one's own deepest fear. To provide that, that is also an act of love. And to give this kind of love . . . well, it is the loneliest sort there is to give.

"My friend," the Swan said to the Priest, "step closer and listen to me. The mums," she whispered, "do not die. The snow does not kill them. You have been looking at the world upside down! If the flowers did not wilt, turn brown, and release their petals in the winter, then their roots, the source of their life, would exhaust themselves and have nothing left in the spring. The snow comes because it has mercy on them: For they cannot bear to give up their beauty, and so the snow takes it from them, so that they are not distracted by their own crimson reflection in the sky.

"Men are disappointed by love because they see only the flower's effort to make itself beautiful, to collect the dew, and keep the bees busy. The annual flowers need this, for their blossoming is the peak of their existence. But one must love the perennials differently."

The Priest turned then to the Monk and whispered, "The angels, they do still speak to us. Why didn't you say so?"

And the Monk said, "Because one needs only to watch the flowers, and to see the rain turn to snow. What more was there to say?"

THE ESCAPE
ARTIST

The escape artist, as he was now known, and had been known for much of his current life, had not always been an escape artist. In fact, he had been a gatekeeper. He was supposed to have stayed a gatekeeper. That was his destiny. His fate as an escape artist was that he would be unable to escape his destiny as a gatekeeper.

On this particular day—the last in his life as an escape artist—the villagers had gathered at the ledge by the ocean's sound to watch the escape artist's most daring and risky feat. He would be tied to an anchor and dropped from the tallest mast of the biggest boat into the ocean.

The spectators rocked back and forth on their feet, watching the escape artist ride calmly out to the boat in a dinghy. He sat facing away from them, his bare shoulders rounded and his head down, as though humbled by something only he could see. The spectators, he knew, did not come because of the chance of his failure: they came because of the possibility of his success. And so did he. Though on this day, what that meant to him and what that meant to them were opposite things. He was not afraid anymore—not of suffocation, or drowning, or being crushed to death. He was not afraid of either the darkness or the light emanating from the woman who stood slightly in front of the others in the crowd, never taking her eyes off his back. He was not afraid of how instinctively his hands had reached to touch her neck, and he was not bound to the world that had seemed to open between them when they had brushed shoulders and exchanged laughter. He was not bound by his desire. This is why he could ride in the dinghy with his back turned and not turn around for even one last glance.

Despite all that he was not afraid of, not bound by, he, nevertheless, found that he was still full of desire and fear, riddled with happiness, and consumed by joy and pain. Oddly, amid it all, he was also heavily grounded by the most confusing sense of completion—confusing, since there was nothing of significance he had actually completed in his life.

The escape artist climbed the ship's mast with deliberate care. He felt the strength of his hands around the handholds and the muscles in his forearm contract, pulling him up with ease and assurance. He paused, turning to the crowd gathered on the pier and smiled—because they had come for the celebration of a miracle, not for the overripe melancholy that actually pumped through the escape artist. He had come to each of his latest escapes as a drunkard anticipating his last drink—hoping that it would be the one that would finally release him, from either consciousness or life. He was naïve enough to hope that release from one entailed release from the other.

Fate and destiny are peculiar things. For one can temper, bend, evade and warp one's destiny so terrifically that it can take lifetimes for it to come to pass—but it will always come to pass, for that is its nature, and it is one's nature, and nature has all the time in the world to realize itself. So, though even masters can tamper with nature to some degree, not even masters can turn something into nothing. And our escape artist, he was a modest man; he was not a master.

But, often, as the escape artist had yet to discover, it is the fact that our destiny will not shake us loose that sets us free to reach it. For some, destiny requires us to fight and tear and rip and strain, and when we are finally exhausted of ourselves and can no longer stand in our own ways, then it welcomes us home. And so it would be for the gatekeeper, who was trying to escape.

Long before the escape artist had become known as such, after he had properly exited his previous life, he had arrived at the gate, on schedule, to begin to fulfill his destiny. In the darkness after his death as the baker's son, after his eyelids were gently closed by the priest, he felt a hand on his shoulder—it was so assured, so calm, that he followed it immediately. He heard a kind voice tell him, then—a voice that must have belonged to the hand on his shoulder—though he could not see to whom it belonged—that he would now move on to be the gatekeeper.

"The gatekeeper?" he said, finally, when the darkness yielded to a hazy dawn.

"Well, a gatekeeper," said the voice. "There is more than one gate, but you will be the keeper of this one."

"And you, where will you go?" the new gatekeeper asked. He opened his eyes (though he did not remember ever closing them) and saw the gates to the park appear before him. Beside him was not a man, or a woman, nor anything with hands at all, but, rather, the most captivatingly white eagle he had ever seen.

"I will go on to the next gate," said the eagle. "For I have a promise to keep and it is time for me to go." From a small basket, woven from what appeared to be spider's silk, the eagle took out a brilliant, glowing white pearl.

"What is that?" gasped the new gatekeeper.

"Hmm," said the eagle, tilting his magnificent beak towards the gate-keeper, "That is what you haven't yet got to lose, that which you don't yet know you don't have, and that which you will have to relinquish in order to use. But all in time, my friend. You have an important job to begin.

"Take care, my friend," he said with hesitation, as though affection nearly compelled him to say more than he should. He paused, stretched his wings and said, "You will grow to love the journeys that people take from the park to the gate. They will become precious to you. Remember that though you may sample their richness, you must take greater care of them than those to whom they belonged. If you see someone whom you have loved here . . . take care, treat them gently; in what you cannot give them, you will find what you need."

With that, the white eagle nimbly picked up the glowing pearl be-tween the sharpest points of his beak and bit down. The young gate-keeper saw only that the space the eagle had been standing in burst into prisms of the whitest lights: so many shades of white!

Three feathers lilted on the air and landed by the gatekeeper's feet. And then, everything was, if not quiet, ordinary. The wind blew the grasses; the sun was out; the park was silent, save for a spider busily mending what appeared to the gatekeeper to be a perfectly intact web.

"I am the new gatekeeper," thought the man who had been merely a baker's son, whose life had, in his mind, been far too plodding and ordinary for destiny or fate to have bothered with. He stood before the stone and metal gate now like a private ready for the front line, the anticipation of fulfillment raising his chest. "So this, this is what I am for!" he thought. It was a great gate. The metal was forged and stretched by the strain of all humanity, and the hinges shrieked at a pitch from before sound had meaning. He felt the surge of what he thought must be the feeling of completion, of belonging to that which is so much greater than he, but yet, that held a place just for him. He had, he realized at that moment, never felt full in his life.

The gatekeeper stood waiting at the gate, but nothing happened. The gate was already open: it is always open, and as far as he could see, no one ever went through it. Eventually, he sat down between the gate's two wings and looked out into the park. He watched the tops of the blades of grass dance for the wind, flirting ruthlessly with it, but never letting go of the earth. He watched the ants weave their intricate patterns across the dirt. He was aware of the spider, who sat stoically watching him from the center of her web.

As the days passed, he began to think again of the life he had left. He remembered much of it, but was struck by the thought that he no longer felt for any of it. He no longer felt much at all, as though he had become merely a filter, through which nothing of substance ever bothered to pass through. He thought of his daughter, whom he had left behind and whom he feared he would miss unbearably, for she was his one creation and the only purpose he could imagine for his existence. He expected, when he thought of her, to feel a terrible aching—a stab in a forgotten wound. He was looking forward to that stab, he realized. But when he thought of the curve of her cheek and of the soft arc of her palms, he felt nothing at all. As if his memories were merely snapshots from a brochure or a play that he had seen long ago.

Since no one seemed to come through the gate, and since he did not know why he stood there, he began to walk. The park seemed suddenly much larger than it first had and utterly empty. He did not see the old man tapping a small tree with his cane or the young dandy dressed as a jester who ran as fast as he could and skidded to a stop two feet from the back of the young girl in the yellow dress—over and over. The young girl bristled each time, but did not turn, for she could see the jester's shadow on the walkway. The gatekeeper walked the park, but he did not see the old woman who sat on a stone bench with a silent canary in a small woven cage. So, of course, he did not see that the arc of her chest was held rigid by the stubborn conviction that she must wait, right there and go no farther. And, he could not know that she was relieved that no one ever asked her why she sat and waited—for it had been so long that she could no longer remember, but since it was the last feeling she had had, she gripped it with all her might and did not move, for fear of losing it.

As the gatekeeper passed between the dandy jester and the young girl, the jester tripped and the girl turned, finally to face him. But neither knew why, and so, without discussing it, the girl returned to the beginning of the walkway and began her walk again. The jester busied himself with the lace on his elegant shoes while he waited for her to go ahead and then ran at her as fast as he could, skidding to a stop two feet from her back.

As the gatekeeper passed by the old woman, her canary, despite himself, let a single trill escape from his throat and flapped his wings. Before the woman could break her posture to see why the little bird had sung, she forgot he had and so resumed her constant waiting.

Upon seeing nothing much to note, other than the many endless turns, hills and valleys of the park, the new gatekeeper found himself back at the gate.

The spider waited and watched him. It often takes the new gatekeepers a long time to see the gate—it takes a long time, a wise man had explained to her so long ago that wise men still appeared on earth, for the human eyes to wear off and for the gatekeepers to learn to see the park and to see the thin tilt in the light through which the souls pass.

The new gatekeeper was growing anxious, the spider could see, and so perhaps it was time. She pumped her web until it swung in exaggerated undulations.

The movement caught the gatekeeper's attention, and he turned to look at her.

"My friend," she said.

"Yes?"

"You do not see the tilt in the light yet, do you?"

"The tilt in the light?"

"Yes, the gate."

"I see the gate plain as day!" said the new gatekeeper.

"Oh, of course," said the spider. "Yes. Well, that, what you see, is merely a safety net—that is not the gate at all. Do you see the child over there?" The spider gestured to a corner of the park that, though the gate-keeper could've sworn he had walked through, seemed entirely new to him now.

"Look in between the light . . . She wears a white blouse and a pale green skirt. Do you see how she walks in circles with her head down, as though she is looking for something, and that tears fall endlessly down her face?"

The gatekeeper squinted his eyes and looked to the new corner of the park. He could see a faint shadow, something darker than the light, but lighter than any other object in his vision. He concentrated hard to hold the shape in his view. And finally, he saw her weaving between the shards of daylight like a dragonfly.

"Talk to her," said the spider quietly. "Walk with her. Take her hand, if she will let you. Since she is looking down, show her the ants and how they make endlessly changing designs. The ants know their duty. Make sure she focuses on the ants, walk with her through the gate and do not let go of her hand. But," the spider added, "walk like you have walked this way a thousand times. Walk without a care in the world: walk so that your confidence blankets her vision."

"But I am not confident at all!" he cried.

"That is no matter," she said straightforwardly. "You feel nothing and can, therefore, feel anything. Here: confidence is warm, but not hot; it moves forward; it is neither heavy nor light. It is the weight, I'd say, of an oar pushing through calm water, or the pull of the hawk's wing through still air. It is even, like the sound of my voice. It is the smell of a room after many people have left but before anyone else enters and it is the rhythm in which the tide endlessly plays the shore. Remember?"

The gatekeeper picked his way through the shadows of the light until he was next to the girl. She did not look up.

"What are you looking for?" he asked, hoping to gain her trust.

"Looking for?" the girl said in panic. "Looking? I don't know. I am looking for something very, very important, but I don't know what it is. Now how will I ever find it if I don't know what it is!" She pinched her eyebrows together, frowned intently and looked back at the ground, tears falling in endless pearls again.

The spider pumped her web again, this time, to get her own attention. She had to stop herself from interrupting. The pulsing of her web calmed her. She must trust, she reminded herself, that the gatekeepers would learn it on their own. For they are not chosen as gatekeepers for no reason, and merely because she has seen them all come and go so many times does not mean that she should scream across the park. This, the wise man also told her. The girl will not be lost; the gatekeeper will see his mistake. So she watched, her many eyes fixed on the new gatekeeper, her many legs nervously weaving intricate patterns in her already intricate web.

The gatekeeper swallowed his breath. He knew he had not said the right thing. So he, too, watched and waited. When the girl had recovered her rhythm of circling and crying, he stepped closer to her. He bent his head to hers as if he too were mesmerized by something on the ground.

"It is right here," he said, trying to keep only the sound that an eagle's wing makes through calm air. "Do you see? They are there, exactly what you are looking for." And the ants, upon hearing their cue, fell into line and danced before the girl and the gatekeeper. They marched so close to one another and with such a quickness, that the gatekeeper took quite a while to realize that they had transformed their linear march into the shape of a small kitten. Those at the tail flicked this way and that. Those at the ear broke formation only to represent a twitch, and those in the middle hummed as though they were the source of all purring.

"Yes, oh, my kitty!" said the girl, the string of tears halting in mid-flow and dangling from her eyes as would the mourning jewels of an Egyptian queen.

The gatekeeper kept his eyes on the ants and reached for the girl's hand. She did not seem to notice, and so he gently began to walk towards the gates. The ants moved their living sculpture with them and the girl followed easily.

The gatekeeper kept walking. "Confident," he thought to himself. "Like the tides play with the shore." And he walked and walked until he saw, between the gates, a flap of light billowing more delicately than any other. It was so very fine, he thought. So very fine! No wonder there are those who miss it. He looked, now, at the girl who was mesmerized by the perfect architecture of the ants. And he wondered what she thought of him.

Before he could ask, however, they had reached the opening in the light and she turned to him and said, "I knew that you would help me find my kitten. Will it be okay to leave you here? I don't think I can take you with me." She reached her arms out to hug him, but the flap of light closed around her, squeezing from her a sphere of pale yellow that streaked towards the ground. Instinctively, the gatekeeper caught it.

As soon as his hands grasped it, he gasped, his jaws twitched, his mouth watered, and his heart pounced on the little yellow sphere, devouring the feeling of small hope fulfilled. He remembered suddenly, not just the time his mother had prepared for him a special meal for his eighth birthday, but also how light and yet full it made him feel. He sank to the ground in the middle of the gates and held the sphere gently in his hands as all his cells gathered round it like birds at a feeder. The sphere, he noticed, was a tiny bit dimmer now than when it had first appeared, and so he put it in his pocket and vowed to save it as a disciplined child would a special candy.

The spider was relieved, and so she began to weave the basket for the new gatekeeper. The light and full feeling remained in the gatekeeper, zipping through his veins as blood had when he was living.

The spider hoped that he would not misplace or mistreat the essence of life that escaped when one passed through the gate. But this was not her worry, and she must, the wise man said, worry about only that which it was hers to worry, and weave only that which the gatekeeper could use. So when his basket of her silk was ready, she gave it to him.

The curtain of light flapped clearly before the gatekeeper now, turning rainbows from nothing. As he watched, many souls rushed through; expelling spheres of ecstasy, fear, joy, pain, but mostly different hues of desire—desire for what was not yet, desire for what had been, desire for the moment that was. And the gatekeeper stood there, in the in-between, grasping for each sphere as though the sky were raining diamonds.

He fingered them in the light and placed them carefully in the basket.

When the curtain was still, and no souls passed through, he wandered the park and came to see that it was filled with people like the little girl in the pale green skirt. So, like an aged host, he guided them one by one to the curtain. Some were eager to be released from the park. Their lives ached in them like broken bones. These, the gatekeeper learned to treasure, for when they crossed the curtain, they released the most sumptuous pleasure.

Most wanted to give up their essence, for it was too ripe and heavy for them to carry anymore and there was great relief in being free of it. Others were afraid, and skeptical. These he had to coax as he had the young girl, and he promised them that he would take good care of what they left behind. The ants would not make their sculpture for everyone, and so the gatekeeper learned to use what was in his basket to help others to the curtain.

For the ones who did not believe, the gatekeeper pulled out the swirling essence of sight left behind by the amateur fortune-tellers. Through it, the skeptical souls could finally glimpse the curtain flickering coquettishly between the gates.

The gatekeeper began to pride himself on his work—for pride, and the sense of a job well done were in no short supply among the colored spheres released by those who passed on. And the gatekeeper took his leisure with them. He had now grown deft and swift at his job. No soul lingered in the park waiting for eternity because that was what they were doing when they died; no young girl turned tearful circles for ages, looking for a lost cat. No one sat for too long paralyzed in regret or anger.

With the young girl's small joy, he went to the old woman who waited with her silent canary on the stone bench. She did not acknowledge the gatekeeper, nor seem to see anyone at all. In her taut line of vision, he held up the tender yellow joy of the first child he had helped across. The old woman smiled and reached out her stiff hand and called out—to the gatekeeper's surprise—"Jacob! I have been waiting for you! You see, I waited, like I promised, so that we can go together." As she stood, following the bright yellow sphere of joy, the canary burst from the cage with a fury and darted across the park and through the curtain. As the curtain embraced the old woman, she left behind a golden sphere in which only the most sublime of completion can be felt.

With a young man's poignant grief, the gatekeeper lured the dandy jester to the gates; with an infant's formless desire; he coaxed a regretful man who walked the same stretch of the park endlessly.

But some souls were more difficult, and it was often they who moved him the most.

To the old man who tapped the tree, he brought joy, innocence, desire, longing and awe, but nothing would lure him from his tapping. Finally, the gatekeeper reached into his basket and brought out the golden sphere of completion. The old man stopped his tapping and gazed into the gatekeeper's hands. He looked up and around the park and then back to the golden sphere. He reached out to take it, but the gatekeeper kept it just out of reach as he lured the old man to the curtain.

As they walked, the old man's face broke open—unable to withstand the strain between his relief and his happiness, and in its place hummed the most blissful peace. "She is here," he said quietly. "She has waited?"

"Yes, she has been waiting for a man named Jacob," the gatekeeper said, for there are neither truths nor lies in the park—only passages.

"I am Jacob," sighed the old man.

When the old man slipped through the tilt in the light, the gatekeeper was surprised at what fell from him: A delightful sphere of swelling, gentle, unscarred love—it was the sort a young man might feel in the first moment he believes he might be able to be a husband to the woman beside him.

He is an old man, thought the gatekeeper; how did he keep it safe from years, from life and from loss? How did it survive?

The gatekeeper touched the sphere timidly, gently, as if he were afraid he might break it. As he let it tickle his bones and lift the corners of his mouth ever so slightly, he thought of his daughter. The sweet, tiny hands that had wrapped around his with the authority of deep trust and total entitlement. She had never held him as though he might break. He smiled. "I am sorry," he said, "that I had to leave you so soon. I am sorry I could not have stayed to know you, could not be there to watch what of your life became the most precious. Perhaps we will meet again here, and you will show me." He could not linger too long in the purity of that love, for the park was filling up again.

When the stoic man dressed in golden robes came to the park, he walked with confident steps as if he knew where he was going. The gatekeeper stopped to watch him and smiled.

The man saw the gatekeeper immediately and said, "This is the park, is it not? And there is a gate through which I must pass. Where is it? I am looking for the gate."

"Well, this is novel," thought the gatekeeper, "a soul who knows where he is and still cannot find his way! I have just the thing for this man who has lived a life in search of wisdom, who believed that he knew the park."

Deep in his basket, underneath the brightly shining love lost, love gained, and desire satisfied, was a small, humble feather—a treasure left behind not by one of the souls that passed by this gatekeeper, but from the explosion through which the white eagle had escaped the gate.

The gatekeeper held the feather up to the man in robes and smiled. The man broke out into laughter and ran, without needing the gatekeeper's guidance, to the gate, and through the curtain. Behind him dropped a tiny dark sphere of fear, but that was all.

The gatekeeper could not help himself—for he believed that it was his duty to collect that which was left behind—and so he picked up the tiny, condensed bit of fear and placed that, too, in his basket. It rushed through his gut like a small fire.

On one particularly quiet day—perhaps it was a new moon on earth, during which souls who are afraid to alight in the darkness rest—the gatekeeper ran his hands over the collection of spheres in his basket, and he allowed the purest of human experience to run its course through his body. He grew drunk on the hundreds of lifetimes that passed through him—first kisses and wondering electric hands, grief so rushing and deep that nothing could stop it, happiness so pure that it sounded more loudly than the grief, tiny moments of pleasure, peace that kisses one's cheek in the breeze, the accumulation of laughter, glances, and shared time that turns, eventually, into its own creature: love. The gatekeeper swayed, dropping his arms to his side, and lost himself in the colors of those who had passed through the curtain.

He almost did not notice, in his reverie, the gentle woman who walked in the sculpted garden of the park. He almost did not recognize her slow deliberate gait or her fingers laden with tenderness as they touched the tulip petals. He almost did not see that her eyes were the same as his and that her mouth seemed bent in the perpetual hint of a smile as his daughter's had been when she was a young girl.

He reached rather unconsciously in his basket and his fingers clutched a sphere of love and of need. He watched his daughter. "So this is it," he thought. And his fingers found the small tight sphere of hope and the gently glowing one of tenderness, and because all of that was too much for him just then, he fumbled around until he found the golden sphere of completion. With that, he walked to his child and stood before her.

"My dear," he said awkwardly. "Why don't you take my hand?"

"Why would I take your hand when these flowers that are already in it are so perfect?"

"I have, my child, anything you might need. What is it you have come here for? What is it that you left behind in your life?"

He remembered the eagle's warning and, as much as it pained him, he wanted for her what was best. He wanted for her to move on. Through the pounding of his heart, however, he could not see clearly what his daughter needed, what would bring her to the curtain—as he could see so easily for all the others.

"If I knew, Papa, I would not linger here among the tulips. But I do not know. I was told, when my eyelids were closed, to come to the park and to find the gate. I was told to wait there, and that I would know what I was to do, when it was time. I was, before I left, so desperate to find you again that leaving life seemed effortless . . ."

"And," he made himself ask, "how was your life? Was it full?"

"Yes," she said, but did not smile. "It was so full that I could stand no more of it."

The gatekeeper eagerly pulled from his basket his treasures, glowing, spinning, vibrating, pulsing, ringing with sound, giving off heat and coolness and caresses and forceful pushes . . . but the girl was captured by none of them.

"Papa," she said, "you show me rocks as if they are secret treasures of the universe. But they are just rocks. I am not interested in rocks. I feel weighted down as it is."

Rocks? thought the gatekeeper, feeling the electrifying buzz of glances between enemies and lovers, and the smells of a forest, the feeling that when the sun sets, one has completed the day as well as one could. Rocks?

He knew he wanted to weep, but his fingers could not find the sphere of helplessness, and so he stood motionless. The curtain flapped, and the park began to fill again with wandering souls.

At last, in a flurry of legs, the spider ran from the comfort of her web and scuttled up the tulip on which the gatekeeper's daughter had fixed her attention. The gatekeeper stood staring, still with dry eyes, at his daughter.

"My friend," said the spider, "you, the mover, the gatekeeper, cannot move. And souls are filling the park here and there is drought of essence in the next world. This cannot go on."

"But how can I be a gatekeeper if, after all of this work, and all of my precious collection, I cannot help my own daughter?"

The spider crawled to the uppermost tip of the tulip, touched her forelegs to the woman's hands, scanned her with her many eyes, gathered her own many parts back into herself, and turned towards the gatekeeper.

"Because, my friend, your daughter did not come here as the others do. She did not come in the false belief that something was lost, when in fact there was something to let loose of. Rather, she came as you came. And now, it is time for you to move on: To go through the curtain yourself and leave the park for her to tend so she may learn to let go of that which she does not yet know she will have."

"So what do I do?" Asked the gatekeeper, one hand involuntarily fingering the uneven slopes on a sphere of despair.

"You must go through the curtain yourself."

The gatekeeper walked with the spider back to the gates. The spider returned to her web and kept herself busy, repairing and tying together ends that had never been loose. She watched from the corner of her eyes.

"Go on," she said finally. "Just walk through."

The gatekeeper stood in the flickering curtain of light and felt a rush pass through his body, as though the wind were carrying him past himself. Just as suddenly, he felt utter stillness, as though the wind had had second thoughts. And, indeed, it had. For the wind that passes between one gate and another can only carry what is truly ready to go. So the wind abandoned the gatekeeper just on the other side.

The gatekeeper saw only a horizon, but nothing before it, as though he were suspended in the sky. From there, the park was not visible at all. In the waves of light that made up the space, he saw, to his utter shock, the transparent shadows of the old woman, the young girl in the green skirt, the old man, the dandy-jester, and all who had come through the curtain—save the stoic man in the golden robes. They did not seem lost now, but rather, they trailed lethargically behind a severe black swan who led them through the horizon's hues of burgundy and grey.

The shadows noticed him all at once and came towards him. Or rather, towards his hands, which held the bulging silken basket tight to his belly. The shadows swooped down one by one and passed over the basket, peering near, but not too close, as if not wanting to spoil a surprise for themselves. The gatekeeper did not want to be afraid, so he kept his hand out of the basket.

At last, the black swan stopped, and the shadows hung behind her like obedient scenery.

"You are not supposed to be here," she said sternly. "What has caused this?"

The gatekeeper did not know where he was supposed to be, or where he was, and certainly he did not know what had caused his misplacement. He shrugged and watched the forms sway peacefully behind the swan.

"Ah," the swan said upon seeing the woven basket pressed against the gatekeeper's belly. She extended her long neck and brought her perfect head down to the bewildered gatekeeper's. The deep blacks of her eyes took on a softness, even a kindness, and she said, "Have you enjoyed what is in the basket?"

"Very much," the gatekeeper said.

"Good. It is important that it is well appreciated—it was the most precious these souls had to offer from their lives. But you cannot take it with you. You have come here, to this waiting aurora, because all that life you are holding makes you too cumbersome to pass through the next gate—and neither you nor these souls is willing to pass on without it. I watch over them until it is time."

"And when," asked the gatekeeper, "will it be time?"

"When what is in the basket fits the lock to the next gate. When that is done, all of these souls will pass through—as will the essences of life they have left in your care."

The gatekeeper stood there, watching the souls dive and dip behind the swan. He thought of his daughter, who fingered the flowers with mindless peace in the park but who could not take her place until he left. He looked in his basket at the rich glowing spheres and asked, "And how will I do that? I am a gatekeeper, not a key maker."

"I cannot tell you that clearly," said the swan with a strange tenor of humility. "The essence of each sphere is buried deep in the memories—as you have seen—and caked in barnacles from lives lived hard. The shape of the key is very fine, and therefore, very hard to get to. It is not easy to scrape away the barnacles without defacing the key. But I can tell you what I do know, which is that the spheres are so heavy with life now, that, so long as you hang on to them, life is where you will have to return."

The gatekeeper kept his grip on the basket, for he could not let it go.

"Close your eyes, and when you wake, you will find yourself back in the world."

The gatekeeper felt the basket grow heavier in his hands; he felt its depth pull against his forearms. His mind sank and sank and the physical world began, like an insistent lover, to touch and stroke his spirit until he reached out to match it, like a reluctant one. On his way into the world, the gatekeeper fixed his mind on the fact that whatever he became, he must empty the spheres in the basket quickly, clean them of all that made them heavy. The heavier with life he became, he determined, the more he would empty the basket. He clenched his eyes shut, setting his mind to his task.

When he awoke, he was midway through a life that teetered constantly on the verge of the ordinary and the extraordinary. At that moment, he also teetered back and forth in a suitcase suspended from a tree limb over a high cliff. The case was bound and locked with an iron chain.

He had made a modest reputation as an escape artist, but he had done nothing much of note: nothing that would echo through the ages.

He swung in the suitcase over the ravine.

He had shown no greatness in acquisitions or skills. Nonetheless, people were fiercely drawn to him as though he held, somewhere deep in his topcoat, the particular secrets around which their particular lives revolved. They came to see his stunts with a fervor that the stunts themselves did not seem to warrant, as if a real miracle might be hidden inside his illusory ones.

The escape artist did not resent these people, or their fervor for him, for he too felt that there was some rippling cache of life that he carried with him, despite himself. He was filled with the most intense experiences of desire, fear, hope, pain, need, and love. In each, lifetimes seemed to reverberate and promise to be revealed. He felt even the tiniest moment—even the scratch of the cricket's legs against his wings, and the lull between the winter and spring—as though it might contain whispers of God. But he could never fully grasp the lifetime in each moment, nor withstand its intensity of joy, fear or love. He knew early in his life that he must rid himself of each aspect that made his life so full.

As the suitcase swung, the escape artist welcomed the fear that wormed its way through him, eating at his integrity like a thousand maggots. And so he stayed, swaying above the cliff's drop so long that the spectators began to grow truly nervous.

When the last particle of oxygen had gone, and with it most of the man's conscious thoughts, he lingered for a moment before releasing himself. For beyond the dark fibers of the canvas he thought he saw a set of gates, which seemed oddly familiar, and on which hung a golden spider who appeared to be watching him. On the ground by the gates, he saw the handle of a basket. He stayed his need to breathe for just long enough to see inside the basket: It was, to his utter dismay, bursting with the most spectacular spheres—their brightness shocked him back to the empty darkness of his suitcase. He gasped, his lungs filling only with rough frustration and the piercing conviction that he must escape. And so he twisted and turned and scraped his shoulders and flanks against the suitcase's hinges until they gave. He emerged from the suitcase and grabbed hold of the tree limb, tired and confused. But the crowd released a loud cheer, and so, for a moment, he thought he had succeeded.

The spider, hanging in her silver web, wondered if he would not have been better off if he had become an ascetic or a monk. No, she thought to herself, he wanted to rid himself of the essences, not bypass them. He did not know from what they distracted him, or what vessel they contaminated. He was neither so humble nor so arrogant to say for certain that they did not distract him from his own soul or contaminate a vessel of gold. There was no way to bypass them.

After each stunt, he devised the next, believing that surely he would stumble upon the one from which he would escape from the over-rich well of lives that seemed to drown his own. If he could escape from a chain-bound suitcase, then he could empty himself of the fear. If he could free himself from the ropes, he could free himself of desire. And if he could withstand the depths of the ocean, then he could live without the woman with whom he believed he shared the most love, and in whose gaze he felt as though there was nothing left to be questioned that couldn't be answered.

And so he hung from cliffs, barricaded himself into mountains, bound himself with ropes.

By the time he climbed aboard the dinghy that would carry him to the awesome *Ouroboros* ship—named for the mythic village that had been in the place of his old town—he was exhausted, but no less full. He felt the strength of the ocean understated in the gentle waves that slapped against the dinghy, reminding it of its slight build. He thought of the basket then, for the first time since the suitcase stunt, as though remembering an indistinctly horrible dream. He looked to the huge mast of the *Ouroboros*, to the confidently blowing sails, and the self-assured ropes, and he thought, "After this, the basket must be empty, for I have nothing more to escape."

He hauled himself aboard the ship. He climbed the ship's mast with deliberate care. He felt the strength of his hands around the handholds as the muscles in his forearm contracted, pulling him up with ease and assurance. He turned to the crowd gathered on the pier and smiled—for they come for the celebration of the possible, not for the beautiful melancholy—the anticipation of relief—that actually propelled him. He climbed as a drunkard drinks what he believes will be his last drink: Hoping, as he swallows, that it will be the one that will finally release him, from either consciousness or life. He was naïve enough to hope that release from one entailed release from the other.

When he reached the lookout, his man was there to help him into his straitjacket. The man hooked the ship's heavy anchor through the escape artist's bound arms, wound the heavy chain once around his neck, banged on the iron with a metal pole so that the spectators could be sure of the anchor's veracity, and nodded to the escape artist. The escape artist walked out on the yardarm like a tightrope walker, the chain swinging behind him like a constant threat. When he reached the edge of the arm, he bowed his head in thanks, raised his head to the sky in prayer, and jumped without looking down.

The water parted for the anchor's weight as a marketplace crowd for royalty. It closed behind him, silencing and stilling the world.

A school of silverfish shimmied and then darted away from him. A marlin slid by with neither speed nor hesitation. The crabs angled away from his feet, but did not run. In the silence of the deep water, nothing moves out of the rhythm dictated by the ocean.

The escape artist was so mesmerized by the perfect pace, the unhurried gills of the fish taking in the ocean according to its rules, that he did not remember that the ocean's time was not his time and that he, in fact, was out of time. The water pushed and pulled his hands, his hair and his jacket with its even pace. The escape artist hung there, above the iron anchor, allowing himself to forget that his ability to remain conscious slid away with the sway of the tide. Before he knew it, he found himself chuckling, for he was floating, despite the anchor. He floated and floated until he found himself washed up on a grassy lawn of an endless park. From his prone state, with the relaxation dripping from him as rain, he saw the gates. And yes, on the ground beside them was a basket that appeared to be pulsing and bursting with the most intense spheres.

The escape artist covered his face with his arms; he rolled over; he buried his head in the grass, and though he closed his eyes, his view did not change: There were the gates, and there was the basket that bulged as big as ever.

From above him, he heard a calm voice say, "Friend, you cannot lie there forever. For that is too long even for this kind of a place. Pick yourself up and go to the gate."

The escape artist did as he was told. He stood over the basket, looked into the reddish purple haze of the horizon, and then saw the thousands of souls still trailing dutifully behind the swan. He dropped his hands to his sides and lowered his head. The cats brushed by him one by one with something between intimidation and acceptance. The swan did not look at him.

"I do not know what to do," said the former escape artist. "I did everything I could to empty myself of this and yet, this basket bulges and pulses and glows as brightly as ever. I cannot go forward with it, and I cannot abandon it, and I cannot go back down and live it again."

"You cannot get rid of that which you have collected," the spider said, pretending to mend a joint in her web. "Especially not that which you have collected from others. They are waiting for you, for you made an implicit promise to help them with that which they could no longer carry." The spider wandered about, touching one seam, then another.

"I know," he said quietly. "But it seems that I do not know how to carry it."

The spider's threads trembled as she zipped with astonishing speed towards the tired gatekeeper, "Do you see the gate?" she whispered intensely.

"Yes, I see it plain as day," replied the gatekeeper. "I am standing in it, am I not?"

"Then, no, my friend," continued the spider, gently waving one leg as though brushing away something unpleasant but tiny, "you do not yet understand the gate.

"You collect these spheres from inside the curtain, drag the basket through the park, feeding off of it and offering it to others; you drag it through life and try to empty it, but it will not empty. Why not?" The spider waited at the edge of her web.

"I don't know," he said humbly.

"It is not yours!" cried the spider. "Is it? The joy? The tears? The ecstasy? The love, that is not yours either, is it? It feels like yours—and the young woman who still stands on the ledge by the sound and watches the night sky—waiting for the escape artist to miraculously rise from the sea—she believes it is his and hers, but it is not.

"So, of course you cannot simply get rid of what it holds. You can run, twist, and escape for a moment, but the fear stays in the basket. The sense of completion belongs to the old woman and to Jacob, and so it stays in the basket. Jacob and the old woman will not let you shrink a lifetime's worth of love down to nothing; they will not let you live it to death in life either. They will grip, lockdown, and clench their teeth shut—and rightly so! So it remains in this basket, as you found it, as they left it, waiting for someone who can make it fit through the next gate so that it will not be lost here in this park."

"And so," asked the gatekeeper forlornly, "what do I do?"

"Well, think clearly, my friend: since you cannot escape it and you cannot make it smaller, it follows quite simply that you will have to make it bigger.

"It is really very logical: Since you carry the basket, you yourself will have to become bigger. The next gate is much larger than this one. You will never make it at your frail size—you will simply fall back down into a life such as the one you just left."

"And," asked the gatekeeper meekly, "how do I become bigger?"

"By becoming more than you are," said the spider, as if it were, indeed, a silly question. With that, she stepped deftly back to the center of her web, curled her feet beneath her, turned her many eyes towards the inside of the park, and took a much needed rest.

The gatekeeper sat with the basket between his legs. He watched the spirits trail like an exotic rainbow behind the swan in the distant haze. He watched the cats watch him and pretend to groom themselves, and he waited.

Finally, not seeing any other way, he picked up the first sphere, glowing orange and full of radiance, and he swallowed it.

The spider sprang up, darted to the edge of her web and cried, "That's right! That's right! It is through you they must pass first."

He felt the spider's encouragement, but he could not hear what she said for his head was filled with a thick summery pleasure. Though he wanted to linger inside of it, he made himself pick up the sphere of pale yellow and swallow that too. Before he submitted to its innocent clarity, he picked up the tender beige sphere. And so he carried on, like a child at an egg-eating contest, until he felt he was bursting—because, of course, he was—and it was unbearable.

"I cannot breathe," he cried, "I cannot breathe!"

"No," said the swan, suddenly so near to the gatekeeper that he could feel the brush of her feathers on his cheek. The brush felt so comforting, as though each feather conducted all tenderness in the world. "No, you cannot," she continued, "and it is okay.

"You don't need the air now. You are like a great fish in the deepest ocean. Everything you need passes through your gills, fills your belly and surrounds you. It is not how much love, or strength, or power you can hold: It is how much of its essence can pass through you. And so the inside and the outside become the same. Keep swimming, my friend. Do not stop swimming. You are a great whale in the calmest depth of the seas. Just keep swimming."

And so the gatekeeper kept swallowing the spheres, filling himself with the stuff of the heavens that had been secured and hidden inside the ordinary souls. He gorged himself on bits of living that were too pure to be contained in any one life until he felt his veins explode, and his own breath pierce his lungs.

The spirits, whose peregrination had previously appeared to be somewhere beyond on the horizon, seemed now to swirl on his fingertips as his own fingerprints. The swan—a tiny, feathered dot—led them in their endless spirals. Only the cats remained outside of him, circling far and then near.

And then—there was no explosion, no blackness, no ecstatic bursting —in the simplest of moments, the gatekeeper came to hear and see nothing, but felt not an ounce of emptiness, and nowhere in him was he too full.

Down below, the woman who believed the love she felt for the man she had known as the escape artist was his and hers only, waited at the edge of the sound. Everyone else had gone home long before. The woman stood and watched the night sky. The escape artist's man had also stayed on the boat, which was still anchored out at sea. He could not bring himself to haul in the anchor—and the body—just yet. They each stood in the quiet of the night, allowing the darkness to stay their sadness for just a while longer, until a golden star gouged the dark blue—and they would both swear later—simply stopped in mid arc, as though it had been caught in a net.

Between the gates, where the gatekeeper had stood, the silver webs of the basket exhaled gently as they received, in place of the hundreds of spheres, one tiny, perfect pearl. This, after all, is what they had been created for. The spider did not need to look to know what her web had finally caught.

The brilliance of the pearl caught the attention of the young woman who had been, for the longest time, stroking the nearby flowers. It was brighter than anything she had ever seen. She shielded her eyes from its glare. The great white eagle heard the basket breathe and swung an arc around the gates to get a look at the new gatekeeper before landing softly between them.

"What is that?" asked the new gatekeeper in awe.

"Hmm," said the eagle peering into the basket and blinking his crystalline eyes, "that is what you haven't yet got to lose, that which you don't yet know you need and that which you will have to relinquish in order to become the gatekeeper. But all in time, my friend. You have an important job to begin." With that, the eagle picked up the pearl, placed it between the sharpest points of his beak and bit down, releasing bright shards of light so that the darkness would have points around which to gather and so the newly freed souls could see.

THE MONK
AND THE
ORCHID

The monk had been sincere and dutiful. He meditated until he was able to travel to distant worlds without leaving his bed. He ate simple meals and did only good deeds. But now, at the midpoint of his life, he found himself unable to shake the words a wise woman said to his mother at his birth. "Your son will do well. But only when the orchid finds itself in its home will his soul be ready to complete itself."

The prophesy had been a mystery to both him and his mother, and he had nearly managed to forget it. Certainly, he did not go about the world searching for orchids. He had, however chosen a monastery in the favorite climate of orchids. Here, he had seen plenty, but all were cut and displayed in vases. He had not yet seen one in the marshes or by the streams, which he presumed, was their proper home.

Every day, the monk walked from the monastery and circled the town—for one must present opportunities for miracles to be born and prophesies to be fulfilled. He did not hope to find the orchid but . . . . one never knew.

This particular afternoon, during the monk's walk, he saw a young woman sitting on the bench by the well. Her head was down, and her hands lay like dead birds in the folds of her dress. She did not look up, though she heard his soft feet on the dry ground and saw the burgundy hem of his robe.

If her troubles had been minor, or if she were pouting out of habit, the monk would have walked on. It was not his job to intervene in the mundane emotional swings of young adults.

But her dejection was so deep that it cut an impassable line across his path, and so he sat down next to her, saying nothing at first.

"Is it not a fine day?" he finally said, without turning to look at her.

"Yes," she said, "I suppose it is. Though I have been looking, and looking for evidence of the fineness of it—I look each day. But the one thing I want, which is very simple, I have yet to find."

"Ah," said the monk. He was glad he had heeded his instinct, for the young woman's weight was indeed honest. "Perhaps you look when you are supposed to feel, and perhaps you feel when you are supposed to see? This is often how we miss what we think we are supposed to find."

When the young woman turned to him, she saw nothing on his face but a simple, pure serenity. He, perceiving her earnestness, turned to face her. She was shockingly beautiful and there was a powerful fire behind her eyes—such a contrast with the small frame and dejected hands, that despite himself, a bolt of physical desire pierced him.

He trapped the essence of it in his belly before it could travel to his mind. When he was certain it would not escape, he asked her, "And what do you think you are looking for?"

She glared at him with the fierceness of a young child perceiving injustice for the first time. "What I am looking for, I have been looking for for as long as I remember." She said. "A flower."

"Ah," said the monk again. "But there are plenty of flowers! Look there," he said, and pointed to the field, which was full of buttercups and lilacs.

"No," she said, and continued to explain only because he was a holy man and might, therefore understand her, "I am looking for one flower. A flower I dreamed of long ago. It was not, I guess, so special in appearance —though it had a purple cone and blue tendrils, and pink petals. But as I walked up to it, it opened before me, like a portal, and I peered inside . . ."

She stopped herself there, sensing that she had said too much.

If she had, however, it hadn't frightened off the monk, who, in truth, understood the problem quite well. "Ah," he said, "I see." He saw how jittery the woman had become, and how the light behind her eyes had begun to spark erratically and so he said then, as gently as he could, "Perhaps, then, could I tell you a story?" She nodded. And so he began:

"A long time ago, before the earth was born from the heavens, there was a sun who wanted very much to have a planet of his own to light. He had learned from the mistakes of past suns that he must temper his desire, for a sun's desire is mighty, indeed. All consuming in fact, which is why we can see our sun so clearly; he has burned everything else in his path. If a sun is rash, and his love blind, he may reach out to touch his beloved, he may want to warm her, to light her, to show her the shadow plays he can make with her world, but before she has a chance to return his gaze, his heat will have devoured her, burned up the lake on which he was to charm her with his display of lights, scorched the trees he was to flirt with her through, and turned to ash the mountains he was to cast grand shadows with.

"As we teach our eager young men when they learn to dance, they must not grip their partners too tightly. So the sun had learned as well, for he had been around for a very long time.

"He was determined, our sun. He had thought for six thousand years of the sort of planet he wanted. He had drawn her in his mind in the minutest detail. He knew that he must learn to control the very fire that would attract her, and he had practiced his dance around those planets who came seeking his light. In time, he learned to skirt them and turn away just in time so as not to damage them, but . . ."

And here, the monk turned away from the young girl, as if he were shy.

"But so much restraint," he continued, "had caused the sun—who prided himself on his extraordinarily bright rays—to dull his tips. And he found that though the planets he courted no longer burned up from his heat, he no longer vibrated and pulsed with his usual intensity. He sent a ball of light to his outermost rays, to report back to him the state of his vitality. They returned, dejected and ashamed and he did not even need to ask them. He knew that the bright, sharp rays for which he was known were withered and blackened at the end. So much so that he could feel his core draining itself, trying to reinvigorate them.

"He sent each planet away, but he was ashamed of himself for having to do so.

"Many years later, another planet approached. This time, he thought, I have learned. I will control myself and sustain the perfect balance between warming her gently and keeping my own fires burning. I will just keep the hottest reaches of my fire to myself.

"And this went well for him for the first few thousand years. She was a fine planet, this one. When her rivers began to boil, or a fire raged uncontrollably in a forest, he coiled his rays in on himself as best he could, and she held herself very still so as not to be pulled into his fire. He was not unhappy, and she did not die. He found however . . ."

The young woman interrupted here, "That his desire only increased, no? He began to feed his own fires?"

"Yes," said the monk. "It was like inhaling the air one has just exhaled, and so he began to burn hotter. He began to wish that he could just explode, releasing all of his heat into the universe once and for all and be done with it. For a while, he was able to protect his planet from himself. At a critical moment, however, when the planet needed just a jolt of warmth to fuel a large rain forest that was going a bit cold, the sun was unable to contain himself; blue fire surged from his core and he was unable to stop it. By the time it actually reached his planet, she was scorched into a lifeless ball of dark matter.

"His heart was broken so badly that he was afraid he would turn to darkness himself. And, we must be honest here, our sun loved his planet, yes, but his sadness at her end turned to heartbreak because he realized that there was no way to relieve himself of himself—not only did the planets die when he did so, but he merely felt emptied—not relieved.

"Nonetheless, being the sun, and having no choice, he was compelled to roam the universe in search of things to warm and light. Though now, he felt imprisoned and cursed by his own nature.

"One evening, as he was drifting about, he saw the most exquisite sight. He could not be certain of what it was—it was not a planet, for sure. Despite himself, the light of his core intensified and his rays radiated more fiercely. This other thing, it pulsed also, but its brightness seemed oddly different. The sun smiled, for he could hardly bear to look upon her for more than a moment—though she was not another sun—for unlike a sun, she did not send rays of light out, but, rather, seemed to gather them within her. The more fiercely the sun projected his rays, the more densely bright the other became.

"He tried to circle closer to her and he heard her whisper that she was the 'moon.'

"He became giddy with excitement, for he did not know what this thing, a 'moon' was, except for that it neither seemed to seek his heat nor shy from it. She seemed to match his radiance, though in a different hue.

"He realized, then, that he wanted her very much, indeed! Like one wants a meal after a fast. And so he spiraled towards her at a furious pace, burning everything in his path. Finally, after many millennia, he burned up so much of his own fire that he had to stop.

"He hung suspended and spent in the sky, and when he looked about, he saw that the moon was exactly the same distance from him as she had been when he first encountered her.

"She simply glowed brighter, and let white, blue and orange hallows ripple from her like giggles through the darkness.

"He shook himself, spraying droplets of fire into the sky. His strongest rays grew stronger and he shed those tentacles of light to which the smaller planets had been drawn. They fell from him as dead leaves.

"If there had been an earth born yet, those on it would have seen trails of light flash and die across the sky. But for now, such visions were lost in darkness.

"He shot off towards her, faster now that he was less encumbered. Again she disappeared from view, until he stopped—and then she reappeared, spinning just out of range.

"This went on for many millennia, until all that was left of the sun was the purest, most radiant, most potent core. And all that was left of the moon was such a deep, pure white, that in places, she appeared to be blue.

"They maintained their exact distance from one another, dancing this way, around the galaxy—the moon gave the sun Mercury and the sun gave the moon Mars. They each placed a light in Orion's belt, Ursa Major, Draco, and the Pleiades. When they were exhausted and had no more constellations to give, they simply fell into their orbits, as if the music were still playing early into the morning of a late night, though there were no more steps to be danced.

"And though they were content, each was a little afraid that there was no more to do—that they had run their course.

"The sun looked over just as the moon was about to fade from his sight, as she did every so often. At such moments, he was often sad, not knowing where the darkness took her or when she might reappear. But this night he watched carefully, and he was overwhelmed by what he saw: As she grew smaller, instead of disappearing into darkness, she turned herself inside out, presenting a brilliant golden core, made from thousands of years of his light. Rather than disappearing into the darkness, she blended in perfectly with the golden rays he threw out into the sky every morning.

"And as the moon descended, she watched the sun release the daylight into the sky, like a magician with a flock of doves, and at his very center glowed the most brilliant white—the same white with which her night stars glowed—though much brighter.

"And they both hung there for a split second, both seeing the limit of themselves in the essence of the other. The sun felt the deep calm of the moon, and the place from which she had sent out those ripples of giggles so many millennia ago. And the moon felt the fierce vibration of the sun's heat.

"In their curious delight, the sun's moon laughed and sent out many colored halos into the sky, and the moon's rays reached out to light them—but they were just out of reach. Exactly there, in the sky between the sun's halos and the moon's rays, a large planet emerged to bridge the distance: She was big and full of the sun's intensity and experimental fire, with waters fast enough to take his heat and not dry up; and she was deep and full enough to echo the laughter of the moon and to hold her serenity without being frozen by it.

"The sun and moon both grew bigger, inhaled as best as celestial bodies can, for the moon could no longer see the sun quite as directly, and the sun, though he tried to see around this earth between them, could see the moon only at rare times. But now, they could finally reach one another through the life they would sustain on this planet between them.

"And the sun, though he was eager to light this new planet, knew that it was time for the moon's breath to bathe it. And so she rose, bidding him to seek his own darkness in her shadow—which she could cast, only because of him.

"And she cooled the earth so that the buds would not burn, and the water would not dry and the ice would hold fast to the glaciers. Just before her coldness stilled the earth too deeply, the sun began to rise over the icy peaks. He warmed the buds that needed life, urged the waters to move, and sparked the incense of those who prayed. And though the sun relished his brightness, the lingering coolness of the moon kept his fire from burning the earth.

"And the only way the sun knew the moon was there," said the monk to the young woman, "was that the waters stilled at night, that the snowy caps of the mountains held fast, that the moisture from the afternoon rains stayed in the dirt, and that the embryos of the young did not burn up with the fire of their own creation.

"Each night when the moon appeared, she lingered in the heat of the sun still radiating from the earth. She smiled as it drew moisture up to thirsty roots, ignited the twinkle of newborns' eyes, made gills expand and retract, and fur and feathers shake for the first time in the dawn.

"From here," the monk said, "at the height of day, the sun still turns bright white, and as the moon lowers herself to the horizon one can see her turn to an orange glow before she disappears into his presence.

"Their greatest pleasure was the essence each shared of the other, but which they could neither exchange nor have. The moon's light cradled the eggs because it was not pure cold and the sun's rays did not burn the embryos because it was not pure heat. And so their essence, because it could never consume itself, kept the glaciers still, and the waters moving, and the fireflies lit, and the wind stirring when it should stir, and still when it should still. And they each orbit now in an ecstatic satisfaction that you and I can only contemplate."

The young woman turned to the monk, and she said, "So I must wait then, to be fulfilled?"

And the monk smiled, and said, "Yes, my dear, you must wait, but so must your flower. But this, you should understand, is not the forestalling of fulfillment, but rather the conditions of it. For you must wait because the flower does not yet exist, and the flower must wait to exist until you are ready to see her. And when you are each ready to give what it is your natures to give and take what it is your natures to take, then you will find one another and open the portal in which you will both see yourself and each other. And until you see in your own reflection the flower you seek, she will not recognize you and she will be unable to show herself.

"So go to the well, and look in . . . there is a flower who has been waiting a long time."

With that, the monk stood and fingered the golden cord at his waist. He turned away from the young woman, and he smiled with the overwhelming delight that is born the moment one finds that for which one never admitted one had been looking.

THE
MADWOMAN

Since the death of his wife, the magic had seemed, to the young magician, rather pointless. After all, what good was it to command small rain clouds, conduct the field crickets like a symphony, or hear the way the moon sang softly to the sun on her ascent if he could not even find his beloved's soul? Surely the universe was not so big? The thought that she would not want to be found was too painful to consider. And in fact, also unlikely, since their spirits had vibrated in such an intense harmony that the flowers fluttered their petals and swooned towards them, hoping to be picked by one lover for the other. But none of the magician's magic enabled him to hear her, feel the breath of her spirit, or speak with her.

So he wandered, as those who are lost begin to do, perhaps hoping he would find her and perhaps just trying to keep moving so that his heart would be distracted by new sights and new children who clapped for his symphonies and his storms. He gathered the stories of each place he visited and listened to them when he was alone. Mostly, he gathered ones that were simple, the sort one might tell to children to teach them a lesson. But these he soon discarded. What he wanted was the love stories, which he took from his bag and cupped to his ear and listened to over and over, wondering if perhaps he collected enough little love stories his own would return to him.

And then he grew tired, as those who are never found by what they seek often begin to do, and so one afternoon, he collapsed at the edge of a small village market. He could not bring himself to listen to another love story, or to gather the villagers for a show, and so he knelt by the fountain in the square. He ignored the children who stared at him and the old man, who seemed to wander the fountain in endless circles with his head raised to the sky. The magician told the fountain of his wife and of his love for her. He pleaded with it to send him some sign that his wife could hear him.

But the water did not break her rhythm and kept sputtering and gently slapping herself, making the magician feel all the more lonely. Just as his melancholy was cresting unbearably, a small sparrow perched on the fountain for a drink and interrupted him. When she had had her fill, she began to sing.

Her song was stunningly simple: one crystal clear note following another, and the magician began to weep. He looked to the sky and gave thanks for such beautiful birds that can serenade even those for whom their song is not intended.

When the sparrow finished her song, she turned to the young magician and she said, "There are always stories. And every story has a place, just as every flower has a bee. And when they are taken from their proper places, the world goes a bit off kilter."

The magician looked at her and tried not to appear as though he, himself, might have displaced any stories.

"And sometimes," the sparrow continued, chirping at a rather high pitch, "the world slides a bit off kilter, and stories fall from their proper places and get jumbled and cannot find their homes even if they are right there. Only the Storytellers know which has actually happened, because only they can tell from which end the threads unravel. Are you a Storyteller?"

The sparrow did not wait for the magician's answer.

"Some people," she continued, "think that they can collect the stories, put them in a canvas bag, and hoard them. They believe that since the stories belong to no one, they can be used by anyone for anything. They think that if they collect enough stories, perhaps they can press them against one another and extrude from them what they have lost. But this is just as wrong as thinking that flowers do not mind if they are never seen by the one they are designed for! It is absurd!"

The magician subtly transferred his canvas bag behind his back. He was quite sure that he did not hoard stories, and he was nearly certain that the ones he did have were strays. He was curious, he thought, only about how he might use them; what they could do, as one might be about a magical herb or an enchanted stone. He was curious only if his own love, that he could no longer find—might be trapped in them. He hadn't meant to disrupt the order of the world.

But now that the sparrow had spoken—one doesn't ignore a sparrow if one is smart—he wasn't sure what he should do with them. He couldn't very well put them back where he had found them, for one he had pulled from the sea in a conch shell, and one had simply been hanging like ripe fruit from a tree with blood red leaves. One of them, though, made him nervous. He had found it on the way into this town and it was, he knew, the story of a storyteller. He was quite sure that he should not hold on too tightly to that one, for risk of smothering it. Besides, since it had its own teller, he was uncertain about how he might use it . . . or if he could . . . or if, perhaps, it had its own purposes. But he was afraid to let it out at all, now that he had it.

The sparrow sighed and cocked her head, seeing something knocking about in the magician's bag as though trying to free itself. She flew behind him and perched atop the bag. The magician turned this way and that but could not see the sparrow stealthily undoing the loose knot at the top of the canvas bag. She peeked in, flew back around the front of the magician and said, "You are lucky; one you have collected has its own teller. She will find her own home."

With that, she released a trill, as a spider releases her web, on which the madwoman rose from the bag. The woman smoothed her tattered robes, looked around, blinked in the light, and smiled when she saw the sparrow.

"Hello, old friend," she said to the sparrow.

The sparrow bowed, as best a sparrow can, with one wing extended in a curtsey. And then, she gestured to the young magician, who was idling somewhere between awe, shame, and intrigue.

The madwoman looked at him and then turned to the sparrow and nodded.

"We have a story for you, then," concluded the sparrow.

"When things are proper in the world," the sparrow began, "there is a place where the very old and the very young can go and pick stories like flowers, to give to whomever they choose, or to take for their own needs. But the world, now, is not in the proper order. And so the story-keepers and the storytellers, well, they are often the first who sense the disorder.

"Long ago, this madwoman told stories that made people see their world differently. Long ago, she made teas to make them experience their world differently. But times have changed, and people are afraid. Fear makes them circle their worlds in tiny steps, as if, by not looking about and stepping only where they have stepped before, they can control what they see. Despite all this, stories are what come to her, and so, as the wind keeps blowing against a wall that has been built, she continues to tell them. No matter how people don't listen. No matter that people seem to fan them away like the heat.

"When this madwoman, who was not always mad," said the sparrow, tipping her beak towards the madwoman, "is seen sitting by the fountain in a daze, not eating or drinking or seeking shelter, she is lost in the place from which stories come, wandering here and there, fingering this one or that one, as overwhelmed as a lone, small child in a landscape of tall prairie flowers.

"When she is seen muttering to herself and yelling in frightening explosions at those who pass by, it is because the stories are swarming down on her like hornets, and she is trying to fight her way through. If she speaks when you pass, you might listen, for she could be taking a sting that was meant for you."

On this particular afternoon, when the magician found the sparrow, or the sparrow found the magician (only the storyteller knows who found whom), the madwoman, once her dress was properly smoothed and her greetings with the sparrow concluded, was indeed, pacing and talking loudly. So the magician took heed and listened.

"There is a madman, now," said the madwoman, who had not always been mad. "Before it was a seamstress," she continued, "or a young boy, or a healer—and when I am lucky," she jerked her head up and around as if hope might fly by just then, "it is a wizard or a particularly observant crane.

"But now," she said, looking at the magician, "it is a madman."

The magician watched her and listened.

"He circles the fountain in the square and he looks to the sky and he smiles and he talks to things no one else can see. Since he is mad, people avoid him and the children mock him in order to divert their fears."

The madwoman herself was walking the square just then—very much like the madman of whom she spoke. She paused in the breaths between images and noted how the families went out of their way to walk around her. The children, however, did not mock her. They just gripped their mother's hands and watched until they were pulled along, away from . . . she didn't know. Away from what, she wondered. Away from me? Away from the stories?

Well, she thought, the stories are desperate to be heard, and desperation makes people wary. They should be more subtle, the stories. They should not spill from me so quickly and so loudly. They should take into account the state of the world! And she grew angry with them for being what they are and for frightening the people away. She knew, however, as did the madman of whom she would speak, that the truth is the truth regardless of the state of the world, and it does not take into account how far off course people have run—which is why the farther away they go the more false it seems to them.

Her musings were interrupted by the image of the madman, which compelled her to speak of what she saw:

"The madman mumbled and paced the square with a disconcertingly erratic gait. One could never quite anticipate in which direction he would lurch next, and so, more often than not, despite one's best efforts, one would find oneself facing his natty beard. Once caught there, in his sour breath, his mumblings all of a sudden became crystal clear—and, despite oneself, one would begin to see the things of which he spoke, as if they were true.

"On this particular day in the square, there was also a little boy who zigzagged around the market in an erratic panic. He was lost and he could not find his brother, with whom he had come to the square to buy white sage for his mother. It was a simple errand, he knew, and all he had to do was keep his eye on his older brother and not get lost. The mother had dressed the older boy in bright orange and told his brother not to lose sight of the orange fabric, and to stay away from the madman in the square. But the boy had forgotten to watch.

"His mistake was as simple as the errand. He had seen the lively purple and yellow cloths in the seamstress's stand and the unsharpened swords for sale by the blacksmith, and he had forgotten to keep his eye on his brother. The blacksmith had allowed him to hold one of the swords and the seamstress to finger the purple silk, and now he wandered around the magnificent square with its magical goods, and the people moved faster and faster—so fast that he could not distinguish one from another, and since he could no longer see his brother's orange clothing anywhere, he did not know where to go.

"And so he did what he had seen his father do when his father was upset or confused. His father would speak, under his breath, to the smoke filing from the incense burner. He would carefully finger his amber beads, and he would kneel before a shelf on which wood, water, fire, earth, and metal were arranged, and then he would bow deferentially to each one. When the father was very upset, the boy had seen him wander into the field behind their house and stand before the moon as if she might take him home. When he killed a deer for supper, he spoke to the deer's body and to the fire over which he cooked it. When he cut the wood for the fire, he spoke to the tree and to the earth from which he took it. The boy had watched him for many years, and he wondered if these things ever spoke back.

"I will tell you," said the madwoman looking all of a sudden sober, "that he also quietly wished, sometimes, in secret, that his father spoke to him more and spoke to him as gently as he did to the trees and fires. But he was only a boy, and only his older brother seemed to take much notice of him.

"So the boy made his way to the incense merchant's booth. He inhaled the musty smoke, and he asked it to ride the wind, find his brother, and tell him that he needed him. He ran back to the blacksmith; to the fruit vendor; to the cabinetmaker—he was very observant you see, and very resourceful.

"He spoke to each element, and he thanked them all for his good home. He asked them to take him to it and to protect him, because the crowd was thinning out now, and the vendors were packing up, and still, he had not found his brother and he did not know his way back.

"He did not know how long his father must have waited for the smoke to return with answers, or for the elements to reveal their secrets. He was certain that the moon had never taken him home, since no matter how long he had stood outside begging her, he always ended up back in their kitchen by morning.

"The boy realized that there was nowhere else to go and that, since the incense vendor had snuffed out the incense and packed up, the smoke would not find him or lead him on his way. He wasn't sure how the other elements would have helped any way. And then, he remembered that there was one element he had forgotten: Water!

"He looked around and saw that his only option was the large fountain in the square, around which the madman made his odd peregrination. But the boy had no choice, for he had to find his brother.

"He ran to the fountain, knelt before it, and he listened to it. He heard the water slip down the stone sculpture and pat itself lightly upon landing. He also heard the uneven steps of the madman, and he tried very hard not to be frightened. He reminded himself what his father had said: One must pray if one wants to find one's way. If the boy had ever wanted to find his way, it was now, before the madman circled all the way around the fountain. So he asked the water to show him the way, to show him where his brother was. But before he could finish, he saw the large bruised shoes by his knees and he smelled a sour air. He stood up, finding himself face to face with the madman, and he froze.

"'Why, boy, are you praying?' asked the madman.

"'I have lost my brother and my way home,' began the boy.

"'No, do not tell me why. There are three kinds of prayer: That which asks, that which thanks, and that which merely acknowledges what is. It is only the third that allows us to run our fingers along the seam that joins real questions to real answers. You think you have lost your brother and your way. So why, then, do you try to talk to the smoke and the metal and the wood and the water?'

"'Because maybe they will help me? Maybe,' the boy said quietly, 'I am lost because I am being punished for forgetting my mother's words, and if I make amends with the elements, they will take pity on me and show me the way home.'

"'Ah,' said the madman, who smiled so clearly that the boy forgot he was supposed to be frightened. 'A long time ago, I lost something too. So I began to wander the world. I tried to cherish everything I encountered, and I looked to the sky, the flowers, the rain and the wind. I thought that if I just appreciated the life I saw around me with enough devotion, that it would return the favor and take me home, wherever that might be. By the time I arrived here, in this village, however, I was very tired, very sick, and my soul felt weak. Here, right here at this fountain, I sat and I asked for whatever gods there were to take me home.

"'But that did not happen. Instead, I met a medicine woman—a seamstress—who could feel how the fabric of the world was sewn together, and who could trace the seams of a person's soul and show them where they were torn and what or who might repair them.

"'I will tell you what she told me, since I believe it to be true—for I felt her fingers trace my own soul with the care of one who has been graced with great love. When she found a loose string, she told me that, since there was no one person in the world to tie it to she would tie it to the tail of a sparrow who flew as far as the wind blew. Eventually, she said, my soul would disperse and be part of everything in the world, and I would be at home. So I wait; I feel the wind, and I smile now knowing that everywhere it goes will someday be my home.

"'Here is what she said to me:

"*It is not so much that the elements and the herbs care if we pray to them—it is not, as some think, that they will be offended if we do not thank them for their uses and their purposes.*

"*The butterfly is exquisite whether or not we tell it so and stop, midwalk, to appreciate it. That the butterfly knows this is evident in the sensual stroke of his wings. For the elements and the herbs, and the butterflies all know why they exist—and despite human presumption, it is not merely to light our fires, heal our illness, and beautify our worlds. No, we pray because we do not know why we exist. To prove to creatures with slighter metaphysical challenges that we deserve to exist. We interrupt the smoke's transcendence by passing it over our heads in prayer; we interrupt the fire, mid-crackle, to thank it for being what it already is; we stand in the stream feeling as though from there, surely, we can speak with God—but all we have done is interrupt the flow of the water. Ours is the existence of trying to learn where in the world home is and how to get there—and acknowledging this is the only prayer that will, in the end, teach us our answer.*

"'Yet people have been praying for thousands of years, lamented the madman, and still we do not know.

"''Why?' asked the boy, 'how could we pray for so long and not have an answer?'

"''Because,' the madman said sadly, 'no one listened to the right thing, no one saw what was in front of him, no one felt the breath of the one speaking to him, and no one spoke the truths that would weave them into the fabric of another. Instead, we looked about the world, to this and to that thing, asking each where home was and if we belonged. And so of course, we never got our answers.

"'When we prayed to the bee to give thanks for the flowers, we saw that the bee paid us no mind. Why? Because it is not the bee's place or purpose to connect with us. The bee finds the most succulent flower and then he dances a dance that other bees understand, and then, they too, collect pollen from the succulent flower, who arose there, just so, to be found by the bees.

"'When we prayed to the tree to ask if her wisdom could teach us where we belonged, she stood silent and still, her branches pointing in a hundred directions. Why? Because trees do not roam and trees do not speak. It is not the tree's business to wander around, wondering if this is the place she should stay, or if she should have golden leaves or purple ones. She is what she is and is connected to that which her spirit is connected. When we pray properly, this is what there is to see. When we ask the right questions, this is the answer.

"'But we did not ask the right questions. The tree has her earth, the flower her bee, but what about us? We kept asking. We saw only that we were not there in the perfection of the word—that the bee did not speak to us, the tree did not lift us up, even the lion did not hunt us, and the smoke did not carry us to the moon no matter how intently we inhaled it. And we were so caught up in what we were not and what we did not have that we did not notice that our kneeling shadow provided a haven for a butterfly escaping from a bird, or a respite for the grass from the heat of the sun. We did not notice that we were the only ones who were awed when the storm winds swept up the rain before it even hit the ground. And we did not see that we were the only ones who noticed that cats often watch squirrels, but do not pounce on them.

"'Most of all, we did not see that the wind swirled about us because he relished that we could be still and see that which he could not. And that we could hear the thunder that could neither hear itself nor be awed by its might, and that we could feel the warmth of the fire, though fire cannot warm itself. So we rose from our prayers, shaking our heads, asking where were our gods? And feeling as though we still had no answer.'

"The madman paused here, hoping he had not lost the boy. 'Do you love your brother?' he asked.

"'Of course!' said the boy, 'more than anyone in the world!'

"'And does he love you?'

"'He says he does. And he plays with me, and he listens to me.'

"'Then there is a thread of your soul that connects you to him, and all you must do is tell yourself a story of when he listened to you so hard that a new fabric was woven between you. Follow that story and you will find your way home to him.'

"The boy felt oddly rich and confused all at once.

"'And so what happened to the medicine woman who showed you how to pray?' asked the boy, who was no longer worried about finding his way home.

"'Well, it turns out that when people did as she told them, and followed the threads of their own souls, they found that they led not just to their own families, but to many, many other souls. This made the people afraid, again, that they would get lost. So, instead of coming to the woman for her stories and her herbs, they began to avoid her. They stopped listening to her and they called her mad.

"'So, one day, she took a pair of scissors and cut the threads that bound her to her form. And it is said that she roams the fields of stories now as a sparrow, whose slight and nimble nature allows her to go where she pleases, and land where it suits her, and sing whether or not anyone listens.'"

The madwoman clapped her hands, startling the magician. With that, she vanished and the sparrow fluttered to the magician's shoulder. She stood there, feeling how his breath strained against his mind. He felt the rhythm of her heartbeat and the slight shift of her wing against his cheek—and flowing from it was a love and a knowledge that was so familiar that he could not bear it, for he was afraid that it would lure his spirit from his body. He tried to keep his breathing steady, so as not to succumb to a hope that he feared would be unfounded. But the sparrow said, "Sometimes, when it appears that something is gone from the world, it is merely on the other side. All one must do then is turn the world inside out to find it. Human love is allowed to flourish because, even though it is only a fragment of real love, it is the only kind that can see the edges of itself and therefore, cherish what it is. It does not easily disintegrate."

She delicately stepped closer to his ear and she whispered to him: "Take care, dear man, of the stories you are told and of those that you weave: Follow the ones that tell of innocence and magic and wisdom and real love and you will see that they all connect—and there, you might find the one you think you have lost."

With that, she flew to the fountain, suddenly singing the most ordinary sparrow's song, as if she were merely a common bird. And the magician, despite himself, struck up the symphony of crickets, carefully picked up his canvas bag, and followed her.

It is said that if one walks to the square on crisp fall nights, when the moon discreetly unveils one sliver of her bright shoulder, and if one presses one's eyes closed at the crest of the cricket's symphony, one can see him sitting there still, smiling perplexedly at a sparrow.

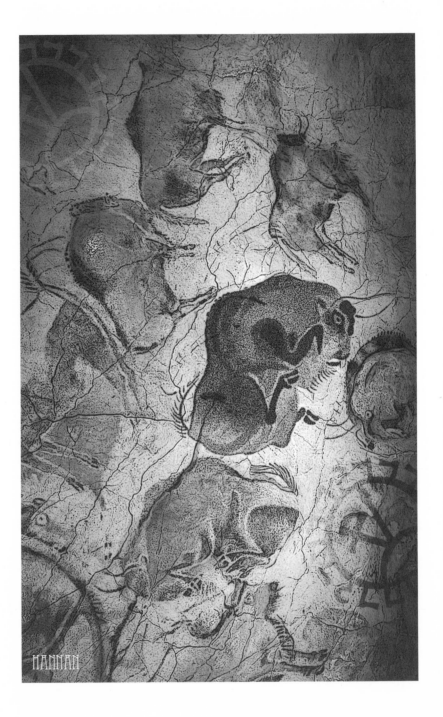

THE
ACCIDENTAL
GODS

In the beginning, the mother said, offering small twigs and dry needles to the already raging fire, there were no stories.

In the dawn of life, there were no symbols. Each particle of life emerged as innocently as the next and, for the most part, none had much care about pulling the What-Had-Happened into the world as though it could thrive or have value for the What-Was-Now-Happening. Nor was any much interested in pulling What-Might-Happen into What-Is-Now-Happening. There was only Now and Not Now. There was only Life and Not Life. Living and Not Living. There was not even, not for any poet's tastes at least, dying. There was only What-Was and What-Was-Not. Now, however, the world is thick with strange ghosts—with Could've's and Should've's, Might-Have-Beens, Might-Be's, Could-Be's and Should-Be's. Now, there is even a place between Life and Not-Life, and a time between Now and Not-Now.

The mother stomped her feet on the dirt, bobbed and weaved her head and waved her hands in front of her face as if she were fending off a swarm of locusts.

In these ghosts, I fear, the Present is tangled and trapped—even the Present of the past and the Past of the future. Can't you hear them whining and whimpering like a wet log in the flames? Even now as we sit here, we would have to concentrate very very hard to see just the Present—and whether or not we would succeed, I do not know. For she has been lost for so long, riding the crests of the stories, finding a present in each one and never knowing which one is truly her.

The mother smiled faintly and sadly just then. As though making an aside to herself, she said, perhaps it is not so much that we can't see the Present anymore; perhaps it is that she can't see us. In any case, now that most things can't be seen as what they are, or rather, do not have the Present illuminating them with her brilliance, the matter of meaning, or interpretation has become very important. Things are no longer just what they are and not what they are not. This you know. The poets—or at least some of them—one might say, are the Present's archeologists, her investigators. The storytellers are her curators, and also her prison guards. Each true symbol is a magnifying glass or a delicate brush or a small chisel that begins to reveal her . . . but there are also many false symbols. And the irony, of course, is that in order to tell the difference between the false and the true ones, you have to already be capable of seeing past them, already have an instinct for the Present.

But let me continue on about how things were before so that you understand the difficulty as clearly as possible.

Again the mother spoke the next bit softly as though it were only for herself:

I suppose it is an ironic truth that now one best approach the Present as though one is stalking her, or chipping away at her encasements with bristles too subtle to feel—so, I must go around through a past so distant from where she is now that she will not see me coming. It is funny that we can be here now and yet still must chase the Present. And so, I must talk about the past, tell stories of their Present and hope that is enough bait for her to settle into her rightful position as the only truth.

As soon as we found fires, we gathered around them and sat together. But in the beginning, there was nothing to tell and no reason to tell anything. Fires were observed, as were the shadows of hands on the ground around them and the ghostly steam of wolves' breath nearby. What would there have been to tell and why tell it? Everything there was to know, to understand, to see, to feel, to hear, to smell was right there. Or rather, right there in front of us was everything there was to know, feel, hear and see. If the shadows of a person's hands took flight, the women at the fire saw this and knew the person's soul was divided. If the shadows took flight and landed on an oak, then, everyone knew that the person had wisdom that those around him did not. If they landed on low brush or nearby on the ground, the person had love, but not for anyone present. If the hunt went well, there was food. If the gathering went well, there were herbs. If no, then no.

I ask: But did not the people want to tell about their days? About the hunt or the treks through the forest? Didn't they want to be known as brave or clever or in need of help? If their hearts had been moved—say by the demure draping of a particular bush, by a mountain lion, or by the compelling contours of another's cheekbones, didn't they want to share themselves with those around them? When they learned that they could hunt with wolves, did they not want to pass this knowledge on? There are so many reasons to tell stories. What of the wisdom of which the shadow-birds told? Wouldn't the wise man want to impart it to those around him?

What happened, the mother said, between the hunters and the animals, and what happened between the gatherers and the herbs were matters for the hunters and the animals and the gatherers and the herbs. What happened between individuals, fire and their souls was a matter between those individuals, that fire and their souls. What have I to know of the man in front of me? What do I have to know that the bison or lack of bison cannot tell me? What do I have to know other than how reverently the hunter makes his prayers over his food, how he pulls the meat from the bones, how penetrating or welcoming his eyes are and how keen or blunt his fingertips? What I need to know of him is nothing he can tell me—it is only what I can see of him.

And of the gatherer, what have I to know? What have I to discover that her choice of herbs cannot tell me? What do I have to understand other than what the herbs show me? What have I to feel towards her that the way in which she keeps sage whole and breaks the lavender isn't more telling? If there are not many herbs or they are herbs that serrate the earth with their deep and tentacled roots, then I know her day was hard, but also successful. I know also that she perseveres. I know also that she can coax and harness strength without breaking it or making it rebel. What I have to know of her, she cannot tell me and I cannot ask of her.

If there is someone who has wisdom that I do not have, all I need to know is that he has the wisdom and I do not. If I do not have it, then I do not have it. All he could tell me—which I would already know—is that he has it. But there is no need to tell me that, since his shadow-bird is in the oak tree. Wisdom cannot be told—it must be followed. That is how one benefits from it. So, there was no need for even the wiseman to speak much.

But you still want to know why we began to tell stories?

Yes.

Why?

So that I can understand them better, I say. So that I can find the true ones in the false ones.

The mother laughs. Heartily. For hours, in fact. When her face finally relaxes back into symmetry, she says to me:

You want me to tell you a story about stories so that you can understand them better?

Yes, I say.

She does not ask me why I want to understand them better.

She does not laugh this time, for she knows I am afflicted with a lethal seriousness. My shadow presses against the ground in sincerity, unaffected by the flickering of the fire.

We must return then to the time I was already speaking of, the time before stories were told—otherwise, our story would have no past, and therefore, no future:

In a time before the first story was told, a boy stands just beyond where the women pass in sweeping circles around the fire, their skirts dancing modestly with the wind so that it will, in turn, keep the flame's attention. In the boy's right hand, he clutches his crippled but sincere attempt at a spear (the wood—respecting both his innocence and the might of grown bison and deer—gave the boy a knotted, bowed branch that would never reach a target). The boy stands there watching as the father walks away from the camp, his feet skimming the leaves and grass with the even familiarity of rabbit's paws and his spear and his arrows hanging obediently vertical at his side. And then the father disappears into the woods. The father returns at dusk, his footfalls heavier, his heart bright, and his palms, knees and elbows painted with soil and blood as though he is being reborn of the earth herself.

When the father comes back from the hunt, the boy wants to know what happened, right? This is what you think must be?

Yes, I say. The father would want to impart his story—himself, his experience and his knowledge, not just to the boy but to those who are to eat what he has so painstakingly caught, killed and brought home.

But no. That is not the case. His experience, his knowledge and the path of the deer, bison or rabbit are all right in front of everyone to see. There is nothing to tell. The boy, he wants to eat. If he wants to know what happened, then he can look at the deer and at the father. If the skin of the father's kill is torn, he struggled. If it is torn at the hips, it means the father lunged like a tiger. If it is torn at the neck, it means the father risked his life to catch it. But mostly, people did not need to think of What-Happened as separate, as something different from What-Is-Now-Happening. That is not how they thought. When they ate meat, they also took in how the meat arrived at their hands.

But what, I ask, if the son wants to know how to kill a deer, what it means to kill a deer?

The deer and the father tell, in their silence, all there is to know about the former. The latter can be heard in the weight of the father's footfalls and in the reverence with which he turns the spit.

So, I ask again because I am persistent to a fault, how did the stories begin?

What I am supposed to say, what the ancestors would have me say—whether or not you could understand it—is that the truth of anything you question is directly in front of you. It is right now. For that is the only place the truth and understanding ever are. Or rather, that is the only place understanding can ever find the truth—though it is far beyond me to know where else the truth may reside. The ancestors would not give you a story about the origin of stories. If it were the origin of stories you were after, they would lock you in the sunlight or in the darkness, they would have you halt, mid step, and not move again till you could see what was in front of you, they would bind you in dusk until you could seduce the dawn into releasing you—but I will not do that. Not because I believe you are incapable of such meditations but, rather, because I believe the darkness and the light too—like the Present—are swirling in the stories told about them, unable to be purely themselves. I am not sure such meditations are as effective as they used to be. Even the dawn can be so enamored by her reflection in what we tell about her that she mistakes our description of her for herself at times. If you find yourself trapped in the dawn, you may very well find yourself in yet another story.

It was with good intention that the stories were born, the mother continues, tamping down a loose coal. But it was also out of weakness, pain and desperation—all things that should never take hold in this world—all things that should drop out of the Present like from a bone-char sieve. Stories offered such things harbor, allowed such things to burrow between our perception and our souls, and eventually, to carve their own tunnels in our minds in which now many creatures have become disoriented and lost. They confuse the Present terribly.

I wanted to ask the Mother, "What, then, is the nature of such things as weakness, pain and desperation? For certainly they exist, no? If they are not to take hold, then what are they there for?" But I did not ask. Not yet.

Would you like me to continue? The mother asked.

In humility, I said nothing and sipped my wine.

OK then. So, here is a story about one of the first stories. We begin the same way I described above: the boy waits, the father hunts, the mothers and sisters wave their skirts in seduction of the fire. But this time, as the sun's rays defer to the grey of dusk, the father emerges back at the camp with nothing. No bloodstains on his cuffs. His footfalls are not heavier on his return with the weight of a soul who gave itself to him. His footfalls are heavy this time with the emptiness of his palms. He sits at the fire over which only herbs and roots boil. His son still grasps his crippled spear and looks at his father with eyes slowed and stretched by spasms of hunger.

The first stories, you know, the first stories were not about saving face or explaining anything. They were neither to share, nor to illuminate. And they definitely were not to create a stage on which Life-That-Was-Not-Lived, two-dimensional life, could have a full and infinite venue. There were no such things then. No such thing even as failure or success. There only was and there was not. The first story came into being in the halting shadows of the wounded—but still living—deer, bear, bison, rabbit, and turkey: in the shadows cast by the continued movement of those who did not feed us. The tempo of the story is dictated by the rhythm their lives resume when we walk hungrily away from them.

The first stories were told because man can be helpless and impotent —but he has a hard time really believing that. Even then, when the Present was naked and seen, man had a hard time seeing himself in it sometimes.

The son, the wives, the sisters, the brothers and the daughters said nothing when the father returned with empty earth-dusted hands. The father looked at them all, and he saw: they were so hungry. Winds herded their intestines into growling tangles and their bellies screamed even though their lips were pressed in silence.

The father was a good man; he did not like to see those he loved in a pain they could not overcome. And because his sense of helplessness was too great for him to bear, he offered them words, since he could offer them no food. He first said, 'My brothers and sisters, today the hoofed and feathered ones had no use for me and did not want to be carried to the other world by you.' The grown-ups nodded and stirred the pot of roots and herbs, looking quizzically at the father—for though they were accustomed to the seasons and to the cycles, they were unaccustomed to the obvious being spoken. But the boy, the boy said quietly, 'But I am so hungry.' His stomach turned in on itself as though it might very well choose him for its dinner. The father heard its threat and winced. He spoke then—he spoke the first story—but it was for the boy's belly, not for the boy.

'I know, my boy,' he said. 'Your stomach is rebelling against the world right now and against what is true of this moment. So listen to this.' As he leaned in, all the people around the fire leaned in, as though he might produce a rabbit hidden in the pouches of his vest. 'When I rounded the tallest pine at the clearing where the bison often graze,' he said— and the boy's stomach rolled as though it were rounding the trunk of a tree—'I saw a small family of bison. The male stood regal, watching, ears riveting this way and that, while the female and the calf grazed in peace. The female was of many babies. She would not have any more and her latest was old enough to fend for itself. She was looking out, out towards the horizon as though her soul were thinking of leaping over it.

'I crept through the grasses like a tiger—so as not to upset the calf nor trouble the male. My arrow shot straight and was met by the beating artery of the old cow, as though she were diving over the last shards of the day's sunlight. She saw me approach, but she did not move because she was ready to go to the other world. I stood over her, caught her blood and mixed it with the earth so that she would know the way home. And I carried her here. Can you smell the skins drying on the line? The mothers, the sisters and brothers have cleaned them so well and they are resting there, stretched and tickled by the wind. And the flanks, look at these! This beautiful muscle and this tender fat! Here, have one!'

The father reached across the fire and pulled What-Was-Not into What-Was. He brought the invisible meat to his nose, inhaled the invisible smell, and offered the invisible morsel to his son's angry stomach.

The son looked perplexed, but he gingerly leaned to his father's cupped hands and sniffed.

'There is nothing there,' he said.

'Ah,' said the father. 'The flanks are not what you need tonight. Perhaps you need something more . . . the heart?' And so the father made intricate motions of cracking open the great beast's ribs and gently pulling away the muscles and tenderly cupping the iron-rich heart. 'Here,' he said. 'Try this.'

The son, now caught in the images his father was creating, now tumbling in his father's own heart's desire, salivated over the metal-rich smell of fire-blessed blood. He smelled the fragrance of Hunger-Abated and his stomach quieted. 'Yes, Father,' he said. 'That is delicious!'

'You can feel how dense it is as you chew it,' said the father intently willing the boy's stomach into submission. 'The strength in the muscles you are eating flow to your own. As the juices drip down your fingers, your stomach is already nourished. It will take a while,' the father continued, 'to digest this meat. It is rich, it is thick, you should feel heavy when you are done.'

The father, the son, the sisters, the brothers and the mother made elaborate prayer to the bison who chose them as her deliverance from this world and who nourished them so that they could stay in it a little longer.

That night, they dreamed of bison running and raising their heads from tall grasses and of smoking meat. Their dreams were so rich and detailed that the growling of their stomachs could not be heard.

That night, the spirit of a cow was born between heaven and earth, fully grown, and fully dead, although it had never been born, never lived and never been killed.

And so, that is how it began—stories, spells, the creation of the world in which the mere image of the real has such weight that it can not only move, it also can move each of us.

And so I ask, "What is the problem? If this is what stories do, quell the raging of bellies the world won't fill, allow fathers to provide what they most desperately want to provide, then what is so terrible?"

That, my dear, is not terrible at all. But what happened after that led us into a precarious new world—some would say, led us astray, but I don't believe that is so. No more so than an acorn sprouting, accidentally, in a small clay pot. We are new creatures to this world: naive, experimental, and trusting. It is a dangerous combination, and probably why cats feel an affinity for us.

And how did we go astray? What is precarious?

It is that we began to live in the stories instead of in the world and to seek from the world the stories we already were familiar with. We began to find the elaborate description of the curves and crispness of the apple, the brightness of its color, more delicious than any actual apple, and the beings who feed us began to seek their destinies in the lyrical bellies of our words, paintings and songs, instead of in our bodies.

The mother poked her stick into the fire to let it breathe. She refilled her cup, sipped and stared at the flames as they shimmied up, as though from nowhere, in the new spaces she had created.

Child, to tell this story, to tell as much truth as there is to tell about it—given the fact that you can't see the truth even though it is right in front of you—is to tell those in our future, the ancestors of those to come after them, the ghosts of our present, that their world is not real. Once it is told, it can't be untold, this story. Do you still want me to tell it?

"Will it make the Present find her way so that she can see us?" I ask. "Will it help us find our ways?"

Oh yes, it will do both those things. But you know not of what you speak. The "Way" I am afraid, it is not at all what you think it is, and that, that right there is the issue. So yes, I will tell the story, but do not expect from it what you imagine it will be. Do not expect from it anything.

OK, I say. Tell me. Tell me how we went astray, how we got lost. I believe the future ancestors would rather begin again as novices than to live as prophets of false gods. So tell me.

Very well. In this version—the version that I hope will be the right medicine for you—the son of the father who came home and fed his family with a story instead of with meat, grew up. As he grew up, he could not shake the power his father's story had had that night they were all so hungry. More than that, he could not shake the fact that, as his father tore the invisible bones apart and handed the boy the heart, he could smell blood and his stomach stopped screaming.

In later years, when the boy appeared in the lake's smooth eyes as a young man, with shoulders that spread wider than his hips and hands that gripped well-made spears with confidence, he saw a young woman who was, to him, of such a delicate beauty and light that even around a fire her figure would cast no shadow. Her soul, he thought, must be weightless!

He wanted her very much. He wanted her to like him very much. He wanted, in the same way his stomach had wanted food the night the father came home with no kill. You see, the organ for wanting—for displacing What-Is with What-Could-Be—though usually killed off quickly in the old world, had been fed that night the father served imaginary bison. And so although What-Was was that the young woman thought the young man interesting but perhaps not as skilled as her proper mate would be, the young man approached her anyway. He had a small rabbit he had snared and he brought it to her, and though she was respectful of the kill and thankful for the rabbit, she was not as impressed with the young man as he wanted her to be.

A rabbit is a good kill, and a precious meat, but it does not take much bravery or sight to catch. Her need for bravery and courage—and not just deftness and speed—plowed tunnels in his heart through which the wind howled just as it had done through his stomach the night his father had come home with nothing. And so, thinking of that time, the young man offered the woman a story, wondering if it might have the same power his father's story had had.

The young man told the woman: 'It was a small rabbit, and rabbits cannot fight, but I had to outfox a wildcat for it.' He slid his hands under the rabbit's supple body so that it draped his palms like a stole. He told her, 'I was hunting the cat, but as I was tracking it and stalking it, I saw how thin its frame was, how hard it was breathing, how weak its heart beat. At first, I thought it was ready to cross over, ready to ride my arrow to the other side, but then I also saw how strong its eyes gripped the light, how decisively its tail swept through the wind, balancing it in this world because it was not willing yet to cross the great divide. The cat salivated desperately for the rabbit,' he said, now placing the rabbit back into its leather pouch. 'And the rabbit nearly stood still, as though it were ready to be caught. The cat, however, could not have caught this rabbit because the winter of his body matched the torrents of snow and he could no longer tell the difference between the two. His weakness was greater than the rabbit's need to be carried to the other side. So I caught the rabbit and prevented the great cat from needlessly wearing out what little energy he had left, and I fulfilled the rabbit's destiny. You see, it was not so simple a hunt.'

The young man stood, waiting for the young woman's eyes to catch on his subtle courage and sight. But they did not. She clenched her jaws and looked far into the snowy woods. The young man knew that to take another's prey was a complicated act. The young man also knew that the story had partially worked, for now the young woman felt the clever tug between What-Is and What-Should-Be, as though in her own soul a distance like that between two trees was forming. She was not sure things had gone for the cat as they should have. This was a new feeling for her. For her, there had been no "should'vs" till then. She stood unsteadily in the thinning of the present. All the young man need do was lessen that tension, offer something to fill the distance between the woman's soul and itself.

So the young man, still holding his leather sack, turned towards the woods where the young woman was looking and said—because he knew his story must fill not her belly but her heart—'I could not take from the cat what he did not have the strength to catch without also leaving him something to restore his energy. I left him my dried deer and my dried bison. I left them for him in the hollow in which he had last seen the rabbit—to thank him for his generosity in giving me the rabbit. And now I give you the rabbit, to honor its readiness to become one with the earth again.'

The young woman, twisting in the confusion of being relieved from an unfamiliar tension, thought this man must be even more brave than any she had ever thought of. He had seen this totally unfamiliar feeling in her and found a remedy! A true Seer, she thought. A Warrior-of-the-Hidden.

And so the two were married.

Many years went by before the wife noticed that though her husband was able to calm the moments of strange, confusing tension between herself and her world—of the sort that occurred the day she met him—such moments happened only around him. It took her many seasons to suspect that her Present—and his—had curled up and tucked itself under the shadows that are created when the light of What-Was-Hoped-For separates from the darkness of What-Was, and that the presence of the man, and the way the man spoke, pried open an ever-increasing valley in which those shadows could stretch and preen.

The young man grew, of course, into a grown man and as he did so, the young woman—who, of course, grew into a grown woman—watched him more carefully. She began to watch what he did as he spoke, what he did before he spoke, and she began to see moments in which his words dangled strangely from his actions, as though they had been ripped into her world from another. She saw that the man was sometimes careless with the sacred duties: sometimes with the killing, with the curing, with the eating of those who had given themselves to them. There were times when his arrow did not shoot straight. There were times when it appeared that anger propelled his feet and hands; there were times when his knife snagged and ripped against that which it was never supposed to have cut. But he kept cutting anyway, as though such snags were the fault of the flesh, the animal, and not of his. She followed him once into the woods—driven by the gap between what she saw and what her sense of the present told her: she saw the time he charged the deer to frighten them. And she saw that once they were frightened, he leapt onto a doe as though he were a tiger and wrestled it to the ground, twisting and flailing, and eventually breaking its neck. But he had had a knife and spear with him. Why did he not use either? The arrow and the spear fly silently so that only the soul can hear them and so that the soul does not become disturbed by the panic of the body. So why, why would he have frightened the deer? Why would he have let her feel his own need, his own desires— creatures die, they die for themselves, not for us. The old practices were careful to preserve this balance. So the man's actions were a painful and disturbing sight, which the woman could now recognize as such because, in her, the space between What-Should-Be and What-Is, was wedged open.

When the woman gently asked the man 'Why?' while turning the spit on which the doe experienced how fiercely one can be shunted from the earth, the man jerked the following story through the Present like a stubborn thread in an elaborate needle point: 'My love, that doe had never mated. She had never felt the power of a male over her and taking her. She never would. She did not want to die silently, and so I gave her a reason to bleat. Her voice had never been heard. Do you understand?'

The woman did not. But she could not undo what had been done. And part of her wondered if, again, the man had seen beyond where she had even thought to look—had braved gullies that even the ancestors had not perceived. She ran her fingers along the seam between the doe's skin and hooves—where strength and vulnerability are joined—the most sensitive part. And because she could not stand upright in the darkness of her blindness, and because his explanation seemed to stabilize her, she said to herself: 'Yes. Yes it is so. My husband helped the doe release herself.' And to the doe, the woman said, as she stroked the joint between the antlers and the soft skin, 'My sweet strong creature, thank you. Your struggle was valiant and true. Your gift to us will be honored so that your soul becomes what it means to be.'

And here, here is the striking thing, *said the mother*: The doe's spirit—which had been turning and twisting like her body on the spit heard the woman's calm words. As it relaxed into the image of itself needing to be wrestled from the world, the muscles on the spit began to fill with juices and loosen from the bones. The doe's spirit, still a little dazed, ran on. It escaped. And so, the meat was sweet and tender when it reached the man's and woman's mouths. It was not poisoned by fear nor made tough by struggle. The man praised things he could not see, and the woman prayed to a doe whom she had just helped become lost.

The woman tasted the flesh, tasted the welcoming moistness and the balance of salt and sugars and wondered if her prayer, if her story to herself and to the doe about What-Was-Supposed-To-Have-Been had not, indeed, made it so.

The man tasted the doe's flesh, watched his wife eat to satiation, felt the meat slide into his belly as though it wanted to be there, and he wondered if his story to his wife about why he killed the doe as he did had made it true—at least for her and the doe.

Neither one of them consulted the doe, who, although released successfully from her body, continued on by wrestling with death for many lives.

After the meal, the woman laid her hand on her husband's. 'I know that you don't know if the doe ever mated,' she said, 'or whether or not she needed to hear her own voice. I also know that she struggled in a way that should have made her meat rancid and rebellious with fear, but that it did not. It was as though when you told me what you told me, it suddenly became the-Way-It-Had-Been. As though one can redo That-Which-Was in the That-Which-Is-Now-Happening simply by putting words together about it. Do you think it also works for

That-Which-Will-Happen?' The wife looked eagerly at the husband, for she was asking about her own soul too, now.

'This is a special and powerful magic. I bet it can,' the husband said.

And indeed, there would soon be a chance to test it out.

The man came to believe in the telling. He came to believe it could change the Present. But remember this, the mother said, pointing a twig at me over the fire, that magic could not change the present, it could only displace her.

When the people in their village needed, the man gathered them around the fire.

They first sat in silence—need was not something adults were accustomed to speaking of. Silence was the place into which what was needed either came to be or in which the need disappeared, and so they sat in silence.

The man waited and watched them. He was eager to help. He spoke what they felt first, 'The land and our skin are dry,' he said, for the drought had gone on to a dangerous degree.

At first they said nothing. They were unaccustomed to speaking the obvious. Why use words for what one can see?

'Wouldn't today be better,' the man said, 'if the gods sweated and made the dew? Can you feel the drops of it hitting your head? Can you feel the toad's skin relax as into the moisture?' The people sat and were confused. They knew that the fire crackled, and that their wells were near empty. They knew their goats were bleating and that their cows produced thin, bitter milk.

'What if I told you,' continued the man, 'that What-Is can be changed?' The children around the fire, lips cracked in dryness, scooted towards the man. The adults traced uneven circles in the dust by their feet. 'There is no water in the well, and the toads are crying,' said one child. 'How can that be changed?'

The wife of the story-telling man was kneeling by the fire, adjusting the coals. She wondered what would happen if they told them of the doe, of the words that could puncture What-Is, stitch together What-Had-Been with What-Should-Be, and create a new tapestry of What-Is. The wife's excitement overwhelmed her and the eagerness of the children encouraged her. 'Listen up brothers and sisters,' she said, the fire consuming her shadow like oxygen, 'there is a new magic my husband has found. But you must believe in it for it to work.' The woman sat cross-legged and told them about the doe's meat and the doe's soul. She told them how their words had—if not undone what had been done—made the Present out of what should've been done, so much so, that even the doe's soul had come to peace.

The adults halted the circles they were drawing in the dust and waited. Finally, one of the old men challenged them, 'Can you tell a story to make it rain?'

The man smiled at his wife. He lowered his chin and spoke. 'See the fire twist,' he said, with such intensity that the fire ducked and swerved around the moisture of his breath, 'that is because the winds are coming. The clouds are hovering over us and are suspended in hammocks our hope makes for them. Can you feel them overhead?' The man breathed on the fire so compellingly that the winds, believing the currents had changed and somehow they had not noticed, followed. The fire flinched this way and that as though trying to find safety in an erratic storm.

The people began to sense a cap on the brightness of the night, as though, indeed, clouds were being strung under the stars. Their thirst grew stronger, the pain of their cracked skin became acute, the need for relief—for What-Wasn't—became great and thudding like a tiger's gait when his prey runs just past his reach.

The children, in whom Need could still rage against That-Which-Was-Possible, began to hear something tickle the leaves of the trees that embraced their camp. One child looked to the other as each heard stems spring against the pelting of heaving drops. The children began to lick their parched lips and rise. As each stood, adults began to hear the rain crescendo like applause.

And so, I ask again, what is the harm here? What has gone wrong? Where is the danger? Was it really raining?

At this question, the mother looked to the sky, gritted her teeth and said with a deep breath: Such a question, 'Was it really raining?'—that sort of question—the mother's mouth pinched in resignation—is only possible because the Present is no longer here, because what is real has become a matter of question, and therefore, a matter of answer; that is, the real is now a matter for haggling. Was it raining? Was water really falling? It is no longer possible to answer that question. The impossibility of an answer to that question arose from the same soil as the question. That is one of the strange things about this magic. It answers questions we did not have and poses questions no one can answer—not even itself.

I can tell you this: most of the villagers who had been around the fire that evening left feeling better, and they slept without feeling the dry sores on their lips and hands. But they awoke with hope—something most of them had never had and something much worse than any cracked skin or thick tongue: something that can desiccate the soul more efficiently than the Sahara sun can mummify a body—hope. I know these days we tend to think of it as a wonderful thing, a blessed state of mind: hope. But from the eyes of the beginning, from the eyes of the first one who Saw, hope is a strange mutation, a disfiguration of something that, in an infant, is correct and beautiful, but in an adult . . .

The old woman paused here, shook her head again, and looked to the sky as she said:

It is hard to describe. It is not so much a retardation as a perversion. It is not that something that was supposed to mature and grow did not, no. It is rather that something that should never have grown grew. It is as though, in hope our umbilical cords swelled and swelled, leaving us passive in the world as a fetus in the womb. The infant does not hope, but it is open to the world and demands from the world because it cannot survive otherwise. It has a primal organ to call from the world what it needs to survive and it expects those needs to be met. But that is because an infant is not truly of the world yet—it is merely in it. An infant is in the world as it was in the womb. The world must come to it. But when we grow, we grow to be part of the world. In the same way the Oak neither expects the sun to shine nor expects it not to, we are not to expect what isn't there: we are, rather, to become part of that which is and that which isn't. If there is no sun, the Oak submits gently, becoming part of decay, part of the darkness. Instead of feeling part of the world of living, it begins to be part of the world of dying. It does not complain about this. It does not wish things were different. The world of decay is as much a part of the Present as the world of growth. When there is only dryness, hope drives us to ask for rain, as though we are helpless infants with our soft mouths at mother's breast. And so, we never think to harvest the dew from the bellies of ferns or to live in dryness as though we were cacti. We never learn how light and frail and still is the world of desiccation. We never learn what it is to be of the world—which is a world of both moisture and dryness . . . Hope is such a strange thing. It stops us from seeing what is, what we are, and what we can do.

And then the mother resumed the story:

I can also tell you this about that evening around the fire: An old man, a young goat, a mature cow, a pregnant woman, and two children stayed by the fire all night, feeling rain pour down on them. They held their bowls out and drank from them until their bladders felt so full, they could take in no more.

In the morning, when the husband and wife came out to check on the coals, the bodies of those who had stayed lay collapsed against the earth, as though if each pore were just vulnerable enough, it could suck whatever moisture from her was there. Their spirits swayed erratically above the bodies as though drunk on a strange elixir, as though the flesh were a well from which they could drink endlessly. The spirits had begun to feed on the flesh. Can you imagine?

The mother poured her wine on the ground in offering, refilled her cup and continued:

The husband and the wife walked silently and hesitantly around the scene at the fire pit. They added fresh logs to the coals. They ran their hands over the bodies that were already succumbing to the ants and beetles, and they said to each one: 'Look to the sky. As the water retreats from the earth, seeking the sun, it makes rainbows appear between earth and heaven!' They described the rainbows for the spirits, whose eyes were fixed on the bodies to whom they had belonged. 'See how it starts just there, in the distance?' The man and the woman pointed and encouraged. The spirits twisted and torqued until they faced the direction to which the husband and wife pointed. 'You see here, at the outer edge,' they continued trying to keep their audience's attention, 'is a deep purple, and then, without even passing through valleys or mountains, one finds oneself in an overwhelming blue.' The wife, as she knelt by the fire and by the bodies who had given themselves to the story about rain, and about rainbows, looked to her husband. 'My dear,' she said, 'what have we done?' The husband said only, 'I think we have made the impossible possible.'

'You are free,' he said to the spirits who were now mesmerized by the arcing colors of the rainbow. As the man and the woman gently separated the coals and quieted the fire, the spirits stayed, hovering like children obediently waiting for the next set of orders. The man and the wife worried that the spirits were not moving on. They should have disappeared over the horizon by now. 'There is no wind that cannot carry you' the man and the wife said. 'And there is no mountain you cannot pass through,' they continued. 'And there is no rain that will not nourish you. You are free!' With that, the spirits drifted away over rainbows that never appeared on earth.

The mother filled her cup again.

This, *she said*, this is where it becomes hard for me to tell. When the man and the woman told the spirits they were free, the spirits spun and fluttered, and one would have thought that they would've gone on, become the wind, become the leaves, become the heat of the fire or the bubbles in the water or the perfect length of the snowshoe rabbit's hock, or perhaps a shade of orange in the sky. But no, they did not. They stayed—neither in the world nor out of the world—dangling from imaginary rainbows. They smiled, those spirits. But it was hard for me to watch.

The spirits believed they were free. They believed the rainbows they hung from were real. They believed they were on the bridge between earth and heaven.

The mother closed her eyes again, as though what she were saying were utterly painful to her. I listened, but still, I did not understand why.

And how were they not? I asked.

Because those rainbows, unlike real rainbows, were between human need, human hope and the earth, the real. Those rainbows were in shadows cast by the tears of confusion the woman had wept when she saw the bodies around the fire and by the light the man's mind gave off to comfort both her and himself. Those rainbows led nowhere. Souls, then like now, do not make distinctions between truth and fiction. That is not their nature. There is no such thing as fiction for them, there is only what there is—for they reenter the heavens as an infant in the world, not of it. And they expect it to be there. It does not occur to them that it might not.

Two things happened after this: as the spirits dangled from imaginary rainbows like abandoned puppets, their bodies relaxed into the death; their eyes rolled upwards towards the clouds and their ligaments and muscles released their bones. When their relatives came to retrieve the bodies, they were shocked at how peacefully they seemed to rest—it was almost, they thought, as though they had, indeed, drunk their fill. The relatives looked in hope at the husband and the wife: 'Can you tell stories,' they asked, 'that will make the pests stop eating the corn? Can you tell me a story to protect me? Can you tell me a story'—said the young boy whose anger tangled so ferociously with his strength that neither could be released—'to make me who I am? Can you tell a story to make the buffalo come?'

That was the first thing that happened. The present had cracked and through her openings, hope, want, desire and their million stories swarmed through like fire ants. But the other thing that happened, the other thing took many generations of even medicine men and seers to understand: those spirits who hung from imaginary rainbows . . . they eventually learned to climb them. They crawled up the arcs and slid back down. They returned in new lives, but—Oh! The mother yelped as though the thought she was having was physically painful—They had never really left and didn't know it! They returned so thirsty. More thirsty than they had ever been before. And that was not all; it was a thirst no water could slake. And they returned with a hunger that neither plant, nor animal sacrifice could sate.

The mother smiled sadly here.

They returned as creatures the world had never seen before—ghosts of their own spirits. When they were reborn, their infant's downy hair, to the shock of the elders, was as white as someone who has exhausted his life, someone very old—as though each were born at the moment of his last death. Or perhaps born in some place between life and death. They were figures of curiosity at first. The kind butcher saw them weakening from lack of nutrition and gave them cuts of meat dressed in fat carved with the most conscious care. The medicine man prepared special teas for them without charge. To these new creatures with the pigment gone from their hair and skin, the meat tasted like straw and did not fill them. In them, the teas moved nothing and could neither quench their thirsts nor right their hearts. As each aged, as each ate and drank, each grew more thirsty and more gaunt.

Why? I asked, because it was the obvious question. Why?

Why? Because their souls left the world by a fiction, on a rainbow created by just hope, lack, and words, and they believed that was reality because they had no such thing as "disbelief." But they never went home, you see? They never went back to their source. The rainbow could not carry the spirits to the soul . . . it could only bring them back down into the world. Body to spirit, spirit to body, but no soul. They climbed up and down a rainbow that never existed, and therefore, never went anywhere. And so when they came back, they sought the energy of the rainbow like a newborn seeks mother's milk—for they believed it was the source of the spirit. They believed that was heaven. And so . . . this is how spirits began to fail to recognize their own souls.

It would have been better if the butcher had welcomed them into his shop and described the meat in detail and what it would taste like when they ate it. . . . It would have been better if the medicine man had stored away the herbs for his real teas and just have given the guests water, telling them of all the things it would do. But neither the butcher nor the medicine man understood these new creatures. How would they have? They had never seen spirits made from merely remembrance and hope. They had never seen skin so sallow that one could nearly see through it.

I began to feel sick here, but I was not sure exactly why. So I asked, Who did give them what they needed? Did anyone?

Remember, the souls had become dependent on the story. *The mother continued.* They believed the arc of the made-up rainbow to be the path to heaven and back. No one could shake them of this (not that anyone tried) because it arose in a place where belief is all there was—there was no such thing as disbelief. And so they sought rainbows made of words, instead of those made of light, water, wind and earth. Do not feel sick: those souls survived. Yes, they found what they needed.

When the pain of hunger crippled them, when they needed love so badly their hearts threatened them, they stumbled, by the instinct to survive, into a clearing in the woods where the children played with make-believe swords, rode horses that galloped on the air between their knees, rocked and fed babies made of straw and served one another tea made of mist.

Remember that though these new kind of spirits needed love, they were no longer able to recognize it in the world because they were searching for something with the resonance of the "heaven" they thought they had been to. They could recognize only a facsimile of love, only a story of it—just as they saw rainbows in the sky only when someone described their arcs to them. At that time, such stories—of both rainbows and love—were hard to come by. Can you imagine their desperation? Can you imagine their relief when they made it to that clearing in the woods?

The mother smiled at me. Directly at me.

There in that clearing, the children broke off crooked branches, skinned the tips with their teeth and strung them up in bows made of belts and vines. They shot imaginary animals and postured against nonexistent foes; they rescued innocents who lay down only in submission to the game and popped up after in glee because the game was successful. There in the clearing, the children fought battles over imaginary women and men, over the impressions of glory, bravery, and betrayal. They married one another in ceremonies that would be undone by dinnertime, and they mourned the loss of brothers who had never existed. And the new spirits, they laughed and clapped and felt like they had found home. This world they understood!

The children heard the applause and became confused: they had expected, at the end of their play, for their mothers to call them home. They had been waiting for the call of reality—but even as darkness settled into the clearing, they could hear nothing over the clapping of the spirits. They were as mesmerized by their new audience as their new audience was by them. That was one of the last moments in which the difference between "practice," which is what the children were engaged in, and "make-believe" held fast.

For the children found that these new creatures—animated by these peculiarly impressionable spirits—could be moved by arrows made only of posture and gesture, and that they could be brought to tears by a love that was mimed. They could be made proud by that which had never happened and could be made full on feasts made of pine-log roasts adorned with acorns and moss. And then, of course, once these new creatures found that the children created worlds they felt at home in, they grew more bold. They began to ask for what they wanted, for that which they were unable to find in the other world: 'Tell me,' said the dying ones, 'about the rainbows.' 'Tell me,' said the curious ones, 'about what is beyond the mountain.' 'Tell me,' said the insecure ones, 'how will I know where the path is?' 'Please,' they said, 'tell us about the love between the delicate maiden and the brusque hunter.' 'Tell us,' they said, 'about the spirit that finds its home—or even one who never does.' 'Tell us,' they said, 'about the movement from darkness to light!' 'Tell us,' said the wisest of them, 'what we really are and where we belong.'

And well, *the mother said*, the children had never felt so important in all their lives. Even the butchering of a chicken—a sacred duty— could not compare to creating worlds with mere gestures and words in which spirits found their ways! No, no chore, no tradition, no practice could compete with this new one. And no magic could compare. They felt as responsible for these new-spirited creatures as a lonely young girl coming across an abandoned owlet. The children found, in this clearing, that they could be healers, warriors, wise-men, sorcerers and gods all in a day.

And so the children became the first story peddlers. They wandered the towns and the valleys and the places in between towns and valleys, looking for those who were nourished more by the story of how a particular rabbit came to be trapped—why, when, by whom and how—than they were by the rabbit's actual flesh.

And so the new-spirited creatures survived. Then they had children of their own, to whom they told the stories they had been told. When one of their children became ill and would not survive, they told him of the rainbows and of the deep colors. They told him that the purple smells of lilies and the blue of lilac and that, if he just follows the arc, he will return home. And so the child did. He smelled lilies and lilacs and found himself riding the crest of the rainbow and then cascading back down to earth: this time, once more removed from the world of souls than his parents and even more enchanted by the arcs of rainbows strung together by words and gestures.

The mother looked away now, her chin down as though someone or something to whom she was submissive rested heavily on the back of her neck.

So you see, *she said*, at first we told stories to others to make the world into what we wanted for those we loved because we could not bear either their suffering or our impotence; and then new kinds of creatures born from those stories began to need them, came into the world believing the essence of reality was made of such things. And we were good. The children were good. And so they gave the new creatures stories. They did not want them to waste away, after all.

But then the story peddlers who had nourished the half-creatures who had gathered around their fires came to wonder, in their quiet moments, if such magic would work on themselves as well. This is when it became a most dangerous magic. Pain, despair, sadness, these exist in the world. They exist like droplets of water falling from the sky and each living creature is bound to be hit by one drop or another as it moves through its lifetime. Such feelings, moments, or their causes are no more special, should be given no more privilege than one drop of rain among billions. But they are less pleasant than rain. I know. So, when the story peddlers began to feel pain, despair, or sadness, they tried their wares on themselves and told themselves stories. This, as I said, was a dangerous magic.

Why? I asked. What was so dangerous if in story, pain, despair and sadness could be herded, could be ushered away, instead of pocking us like hail? What if one could shoo them on their ways with a few words? What is the harm in that?

Because that is not what happens—although it may feel as though that is what is happening.

And so, and so, the droplets of pain, *the mother continued*—instead of evaporating in submission to the Present, in whom nothing but itself can last—took hold in the story in which pain leads to something else. One droplet spread and multiplied until it became a river that wound around the curves of deeper suffering, trickled over regret, slid down resignation and finally pooled in something like growth or strength. A river that no one has been able to dam since. And so, instead of passing through one droplet of pain, the storytellers and the story listeners began to experience the powerful current of the river—and therefore, they never learned to feel pain as just itself. And the same is true of despair. Instead of being discarded by the Present as a mutation of nature, an entity that could never survive life—the minor stumble, from which one should have regained balance with one's next step, became a well from which one could only be pulled by another. And so now, those who encounter despair do not just encounter one droplet of time from which they can walk on, nor one depression in the earth over which they might stumble for a moment. No, instead of passing by, or through, they are mired in the sling of an upside-down rainbow, waiting and waiting for comfort to happen by and free them. A frightfully difficult task.

But, since the story peddlers must be attentive to the needs of their consumers, there are also stories for such difficulties. Stories about fortune, stories about fate; they carve inexorable valleys between What-Was and What-Was-Wanted, and so those in the slings of the upside-down rainbows can believe they are right-side up, for a while at least.

Here in these slings, fear finds itself married to overcoming and love to loss. Death, instead of being able to be itself, finds itself in tight bondage with life. Lions find themselves caged in cities; ravens perch on arms instead of branches, and the dawn lifts her lashed lids in the middle of the night while the moon finds herself shining abashedly when the sun is still at high noon. Lions, instead of just being majestic, come to look for their reflections in the awe of men. Cranes, instead of being serenity and strength, come to ponds, to admire the reflection of serenity and strength. And ponds . . . oh. Ponds pool in the earth to reflect the sun, to be the places of gathering for cranes and egrets and monks. And they forget, they forget, that the reason they ever held such honor in the first place is because they did not know it and, like the Present, only reflected what the light gave them.

And so the storytellers learned and taught to others that what they could not see could be created through stories, that survival was not in the world, not in finding their place in the world, but was, rather, in the stories they could tell about themselves and the world. One could die in such survival and, if one was a good enough storyteller, never even know it.

And the Present, I ask. What happened to her?

To my shock, tears began to crash down the mother's face like a crystal cave collapsing.

The Present? *She sighed deeply.* The Present now, if you want to go looking, is the place in a story, or in the story the world has become, or in the world the story has become, in which despair succumbs to her and evaporates, in which there is no river for pain to gain current in; in which the arm on which the raven perches is, in fact, a branch, in which the pond is just the pond, and the lion does not recognize the size of his mane in our awe of it, but rather in how it holds back the wind when he charges and catches the scent of the lioness in the wind. In such moments, one can find the rune in the pile of unmarked rocks. When one can watch the lion without wondering how he got there, where he is going, or what he means, then, one is coming closer to the Present.

But you, my precious dear—unlike those of us who are merely accidental gods—you will only find yourself if you stop looking. Stop looking for yourself. You are not in the world, you are the time in which the world takes place. I am not your pond. You are everywhere, at all times and no-time; that is what you are. It is our job to look for you, not yours to look for us. You will not find yourself in the stories about yourself. You do not exist on that imaginary rainbow. You will, in fact, never "find" yourself. We can lose you, and you can get lost in us, but you cannot find yourself in us—not anymore at least. Whether or not you will return to us so that we can see ourselves, see the world clearly, is a matter not of what you are told, nor of what you tell, but, rather, of when you come to exist again solely as yourself—living and riding rainbows that emerge from heat, sun, rain and earth.

Things in the Present do not stand for other things; each thing is itself. This—do not rush your thoughts—is less a matter of things, and more a matter of standing. The owl flying west in daylight is always an owl flying west in daylight. This is what the owl flying west in daylight means—but now, it is much harder to know the owl or the west or the flying or the daylight as themselves. And so we lose the owl. And so we lose her flight. And so we must 'make' meaning of those things as though it is up to us.

And so what would it have meant back then when things were themselves and did not stand for other things, when the Present was present?

The mother laughed here. What would it have meant? My dear, I can't tell you that. I can tell you stories about what it could mean. Which story would you like? If I am in the scene, if I am the one who sees the owl and it is to my west that she flies? On which day? Which month? What is my present? You see? To see what something is as itself is to take a very long view. The present expands eternally before one like the owl's wings under the sun.

Perhaps though, *and here the mother ran her fingers along the ceramic lip of her cup,* perhaps what you are asking is for me to articulate the difference between what I might have seen, that kind of thing, and what people are most likely now to see?

Yes, I say. If that is as close as I can get to it, then yes. Perhaps understanding of the sort I need is also a bit like the Present—it must be courted from a distance, stalked with stealth so that it does not fear being imprisoned. So yes.

OK. Now, people might see the owl flying west in the daytime as, perhaps, a story for you, a symbol for you, a message. You tell me what the message might be.

Well, I say, feeling my words and thoughts becoming thin and flimsy as wet rice paper, perhaps I would think it means I am to die soon. To enter the west gate. Perhaps it means to warn or to prepare me. The owl sees between life and death. The west is its home and the west is death's gate. Day is not the time of the owl, so perhaps it means I have risk of dying in the light, when it is not my time.

The mother sipped her wine. That is very good. That is poetic like a flute song caressing low-hanging mist until it forms the shapes of lotuses or dragons. There is beauty in the symbols of stories. Much much beauty. I see why so many live only in them and only according to them—perhaps the Present is not so much trapped in them as she has been seduced by them.

The mother rubbed her fingers along the corners of her eyes, watched the flames of the fire play hide-and-seek under the logs, nannied by the coals, and she said: I, were I in the Present, would not have said to myself that the west meant anything other than the west. Nor that the owl meant anything other than an owl. I would not have had to. I would have had an experience of the fullness of each—like watching a trickle of water find its way into a canal. Not that anything would be, or was supposed to be, or wasn't supposed to be. Whatever was just was, right then. I would no more have thought there was something to be warned of, to run towards or away from than the trickle of water that finds itself at the opening of a small canal can turn back. I do not know how else to say this: to those who were in the Present when she was still able to find us, the west was the west and the owl was the owl—in all of their expansiveness. The west did not stand for anything: it Was everything and more than people now think "the west" might mean. And the owl, she did not represent anything; she Was the things you say she represents. But that was a long time ago. Now, who knows where the real owls are or where the west is. It is a wonder the sun doesn't get confused and the poles do not slide and tumble around one another like bears fighting.

And then the mother said: Look at your shadow. It clings to the ground and does not move. Why do you think that is?

I was caught, here, I confess. I did not know and I did not know what to ask.

Your shadow cannot leave the fire because you do not exist in time—you exist in between it. You exist only here, only now. But you strain against this and drain the fire. You are trying to make your shadow move.

One thing did not stand for another when the Present was present, not because it was impossible, but simply because where it was possible, there was no need: each thing already was, or contained or reflected the thing it would stand for, were there any need for one thing to be represented as the other. Don't you remember? It is your job to stand between the two—the reality and the telling of it—so that the one never gets confused with another—so that no thing believes it must become something else to reveal either's truth. You do not need a shadow to understand yourself; you need to be the space in which shadows are just shadows.

THE
MEDICINE
TRILOGY

One Death

The Autumn Cicada Dies
By the side of its empty shell

Naitō Jōsō

One dies a million deaths in the course of one life. In one death, one can also live a million lives. But we will not discuss them all. We will have to pick and choose in order to make our point. We ask forgiveness from the lives we are excluding. We do not mean to make less of them. It is simply that that is the way with points one has to make: Some things, and in this case, some lives, must hover in the shadows—but shadows are made to harbor such things. That is the way, and that is the agreement.

The sun beats down on the plain. They run as fast as they can, and the sun runs through the follicles of their hairs like messages down telephone wire, letting each know the whole of which it is a part, leading each to its position in the sweep of the group across the valleys and the hills. The

115

echo of their hooves pounding against the dry earth drives them on like warrior drums. But some of them fall anyway, for that is the way, and that was the agreement. We could never have conquered them on our own, but some of them agreed to fall. And so, down they went.

Smaller creatures slide over snow like ribbons around a girl's wrist. They hunch their backs against the bases of trees, and they forage tirelessly for their own survival, living lives of pure gentleness, occasionally stopping to find their likenesses in small shrubs crouching under snow-blankets. But some of them fall anyway, for that is the way, and that was the agreement. Our traps would never have deceived them had they not agreed to be held fast in the snow, gripped by metal teeth. But some of them did agree.

Others live high above them, armed with senses so sharp that the densely complicated earth appears to them as an ornate—but transparent —atmosphere, and neither distance nor time binds the sounds they can hear and the sights they can see. Despite the paucity of our form in comparison with theirs, some of them come to us, respond to us, allow us to borrow their majesty. For that, too, is the way and was the agreement.

All those who fall, are trapped, or are borrowed from are honored in a way the living can only hope for. And finally, when the meat is cured, when the blood is mixed with herbs for medicine, when the skin is harvested for those of us whose skin does not protect us, when the bones reveal their secrets and the hair its perception, those who have drawn up the agreement are satisfied and those who eat the meat, use the medicine, wear the skin and hear the secrets whispered in their ears smile in admiration, in awe of those between whom the agreement has been made.

Some of them pray in simple gratitude.

Some of them in gracious gratitude.

Some of them in awe.

And some of them, often those who mix the medicine or draw the secrets from the honest bones, allow themselves to wonder—in the secret pockets of sacredness their work provides—what it would mean, what it would take, to become part of the agreement making, and not just the recipients of it.

They taste the blood.

They suck the marrow from the bones.

Horns are caressed and the roots of feathers are made to sing.

This is part of the agreement.

Some of us, we who are the recipients of the agreement, we run too. We run, but we do not make drums with our feet to unite and propel us; no, we use the thunder for that, and the percussion of the crows and woodpeckers, and the vibration of the herds. And some of us fall, for that is the way. Though, since we are not in on the agreement, some of us do not know why we fall. We think the most painful thoughts at the moment of transition, that something has gone wrong, that we have done wrong, that someone else has done wrong, but surely—our pain confuses us—someone has done wrong. Those of us return—the first arbiters of justice— looking to right the wrongs, to right the source of the wrongs, not the wrongdoer—and that, by the way, is how one distinguishes witches (of the bad sort) from sages—the former seek revenge, the latter seek to heal the wound that caused the injustice—so we new ones are reborn, infants among newborns, we know we are limited, can only see through the prisms of certain gems. So some of us choose physical ails, others of us choose emotional ails, and others of us spiritual ails. We return, as seekers—and as potential healers—suspicious of the agreement. In the very first round, those who return to find out why we fall discover records of the agreements between time and space, between the wind and the mountains, between particular herbs and a particular microorganism.

One evening, in the dawn of these times, one man prepares the skull of a great grizzly who has given himself to the conviction of a young hunter's first well-shot arrow. Instead of just cleaning the skull, however, the man—a special man, for only Seers, those with a certain respect for the agreement, are given the duty to prepare skulls—fits the massive structure to his own crown. He carefully pulls it down over his hair and adjusts the angle of it so that his own eyes look out through the sockets. He knows the bears are part of those in on agreement making, and for just a moment, he wonders what the bear sees that he cannot. When he looks through the skull, he does not see anything unusual, but at night, he dreams the strangest dream.

In it, all the world appears first as he knows it; grasses grow up from plains, flowers allow bees to tickle their hearts, waters relentlessly carve grooves in the earth and then recline in them, as though obediently following someone else's fervor. Lions eat bison and gazelles. Wolves eat rabbits and rabbits eat the grass that grows up from the plains and deer droppings give the skirted plains the energy to make their skirts dance. But then the dream shifts, and instead of the clean, simple line of agreements linking each thing in the familiar chain, everything starts to move—soil, flowers, birds, snakes, rock formations, ice caps, lions, buffalo, cats, ravens, whales—at the same time, as though the agreements are being blasted by some invisible force underneath them.

The movement swirls in all directions like tornadoes gyroscoping inside tornadoes: The eagles come from the heavens, to be sure, and the cats shadow walk—not between above and below—but between here and there, sideways. The snakes rise from the earth, to be sure; the ravens call out the darkness from the light and the lightness from the dark, and the vultures carry the earth to the heaven by purifying it, to be sure. Each carries her messages and his medicines. But those are only the big movers. Silent and tiny transactions between the creatures who exist mostly for their prey or for their predator, or who are so specialized that even most of the animal kingdom does not bother with them, swirl like particles of dust, making up the majority of the vortex, nearly unnoticed by all. The Seer is dizzied by the movements of it all. And then the focus of the dream shifts again, this time in eagle-eyed corradiation on one of those swirling particles: One squirrel sits in relative safety by an oak, devotedly gnawing an acorn. Off to his left—he is always alert—there is a small beetle, his waving legs and thrashing head are the only indication of his panic. The squirrel continues with his nut, and the beetle struggles upside down, trapped between stones so tiny that a rabbit's paw would not feel them. In this particle of the tornado—invisible to most eyes—the squirrel, neither predator nor prey to this creature, with no perceptual faculties to feel his panic, nonetheless tucks his nut into his cheek, scampers to the beetle, stands over him for one instant, thumps his tail once, and with his tiny paw, he moves the tiny stone and rights the beetle—perhaps by accident. The beetle gathers his legs under him, feels them support his barge of a body, and walks quite elegantly onto a nearby oak leaf, where he rests until the hairs on his legs and his antennae alert him to an ant who has fallen during his rounds and is ready to be broken down for the earth to digest him.

The Seer wakes, awed and confused by the dream, and in particular, by the last few moments of the dream. Of course what the squirrel did was not an act of compassion. The Seer is not in the habit of importing human experiences onto the animal world. But it was still something. Something devoid of the emotional content of love, devoid of intention to heal, or to save another, or to salvage ones own soul—surely the squirrel did not possess those things, and surely the beetle's specialized antennae would not have recognized them even if he had. But it was still something—something that looked very much like love and compassion. Perhaps, thought the Seer when he awoke, love is not some grand heavenly music played only for and by the greatest musicians. Perhaps it is made up like that music of tiny, nearly unrecognizable particles that share, on their own, no resemblance to this thing human beings look for and feel.

Perhaps, one act like that, accumulated over the evolution of a soul—in the move from beetle to butterfly, from spider to mouse—each receiving what it is capable of perceiving and no more, perhaps the soul starts to put the pieces together, adds the particles, and at the end, at the end it looks like the harmony and adherence we think of as love. Perhaps, he thought to himself and smiled, we humans actually perceive only the coarsest, most obvious masses of love—perhaps, he laughed out loud, our perceptive faculties are so unrefined and immature that we can only feel love when it is at its biggest sizes and in its most crude manifestations. "Well," he thought, "that would explain why we are not in on the agreement! We are too immature yet. But bless them for allowing us to be recipients of the agreement."

One dies a million deaths in the course of one life. In one death, one can also live a million lives.

The man lies face up in the snow, dying. For a moment, he thinks he will appreciate, finally, the sun—and perhaps the ice! For the ice is a fine reflector. Perhaps, thinks the man, the only thing that can reflect the majesty of the sun—for water has its own vanity, and therefore, interrupts the light with her swaying, her many decorations, and her ever-changing colors. But the ice, thinks the man, the ice is the most humble of the elements. Going nowhere fast, needing no decoration, devoid of vanity, despite its pure beauty. Perhaps, he thinks, this is what I will come to appreciate as I die. For he believes that in death, in the evaporation of the need to move, to go on, of one's own vanity, one might see things in a different light. One might be awed.

He waits for the awe. He waits through the early hours of the dark morning before he dies. He waits to feel the sun slip in between the ice and the skin of his neck, his arms, his feet. He knows the ice does not cling to him, it merely cradles him and holds him still; there is plenty of room for the sun to get in. He allows himself to wonder, even, if this will not be his moment of enlightenment. Will the wonders of the world not dawn on him as the sun—the sun who sees half of everything and is told of the other half by the moon as they pass one another each day—sees him one last time. Maybe an eagle will fly overhead. Maybe a snowshoe rabbit will kiss him. Maybe a lone wolf will appear at his feet, look him directly in the eyes, and sit with him so that neither of them will be alone.

As dawn comes, he feels little pain—he feels little of anything anymore, except a heaviness in his chest. He waits for the sun.

But it is a cloudy day.

The sun is preening himself behind the thick protection of clouds that will not dance with the wind until nearly nightfall. It is a day for the ice to stay itself a little while longer and a day that will be safer for the gray rabbits to forage in camouflage. They will not, however, venture to the middle of the cliff where the man lies. The wolves will not, therefore, follow their tracks and appear at the feet of the man, and the eagle is already back in his nest, his peacefully closed lids belying his regal talons and beak.

When the man finally finishes dying, the ice that has melted from the heat of his body regathers itself, resuming its position as though he had never been there.

The sun radiates across the plain. The hoofed ones run as fast as they can. They feed on one another's energy and the sun courses through the follicles of their hairs like messages down telephone wire. The echo of their hooves pounding against the dry ground drives them on like warrior drums. But some of them fall anyway, for that is the way, and that was the agreement. We could never have conquered them on our own, but some of them agreed to fall. And so, down they went.

Smaller creatures slide over snow like ribbons around a girl's wrist, they hunch their backs against the base of trees and they forage tirelessly for their own survival, living lives of pure gentleness and stopping, occasionally, to recognize their likenesses in the shrubs that crouch under snow-blankets. But some of them fall anyway, for that is the way, and that was the agreement. Our traps would never have deceived them had they not agreed to be held fast in the snow, gripped by metal teeth. But some of them did agree.

Others live high above them, armed with senses so sharp the thick and complicated earth appears to them as an ornately decorated onion skin, and neither distance nor time are a boundary to the sounds they can hear and the sights they can see. Despite the paucity of our form in comparison with theirs, some of them come to us, respond to us, allow us to borrow their majesty. For that too, was the way and the agreement.

All those who fell, were trapped, or were borrowed from were honored in a way the living can only hope for. And finally, when the meat was cured, when the blood was mixed with herbs for medicine, when the skin was harvested for those of us whose skin does not protect us, when the bones revealed their secrets and the hair its perception, those who drew up the agreement were satisfied and those who ate the meat, used the medicine, wore the skin and heard the secrets whispered in their ears smiled in admiration, in awe of those between whom the agreement had been made.

Some of them prayed in simple gratitude.

Some of them in gracious gratitude.

Some of them in awe.

And some of them, often those who mixed the medicine or drew the secrets from the honest bones, allowed themselves—in the secret pockets of sacredness their work provided—to wonder what it would mean, what it would take, to become part of the agreement making, and not just the recipients of it.

They tasted the blood.

They sucked the marrow from the bones.

Horns were caressed and the roots of feathers were made to sing.

This was part of the agreement.

One morning, in the afternoon of these times, one man was preparing the skull of a great grizzly who had given himself to the flight of a young hunter's first well-shot arrow and who had died singing praise of the boy's conviction. Instead of just cleaning the skull, however, the man—a special man, for only Seers are given the duty to prepare skulls—fitted the massive structure to his own crown. He carefully pulled it down over his hair and adjusted the angle of it so that his own eyes looked out through the sockets.

That night, he dreamed the strangest dream: In it, all the world moved —soil, flowers, birds, snakes, rock formations, ice caps, lions, buffalo, cats, ravens, whales—at the same time, in an indecipherable choreography. The movement traveled in all directions like tornadoes inside tornadoes: the eagles came from the heavens, to be sure, and the cats shadow-walked— not between above and below—but between here and there, sideways. The snakes rose from the earth, to be sure, and the ravens called out the darkness from the light and the lightness from the dark. Each carried her messages and his medicines. But those were only the big movers. Silent and tiny transactions between the creatures who exist mostly for their prey or for their predator, or who are so specialized that even most of the animal kingdom does not bother with them, swirled like particles of dust, making up the majority of the vortex, nearly unnoticed by all. The Seer was dizzied by the movements. And then the dream shifted, this time in eagle-eyed focus on one of those swirling particles: A human lay dying face up in a deep snow drift on a steep cliff. He was cradled by a million particles of water who had stilled themselves to hold him. He was stiff, his face pinched by the concentration of the cold against his skin. His blood, upon registering that he was dying, ran through his veins faster than ever—not to save him, not to protect his organs, but to scavenge the heat from the fission of soul and body—for there was an agreement too between this man's blood and something else in the world. But then the dream shifted again—from the blood to the man himself. The man tried to clench his fists. With the force of desperate anger, he pulled the heat back from his veins into his mind to think one last thought: "Why? I do not understand!" The ice turned dark around him, as though refusing to reflect the light of the sun, as though it were, instead, absorbing the isolation, the feeling that the world had abandoned the man.

And then the Seer followed this man as he pushed against the ice, pushed against his body and muscled his way out of his life in a fit of confusion, betrayal and anger. The Seer watched the trail the heat from the blood was supposed to have cut through the ice, he saw the krill who would not be freed from a thread of ice-algae it had gotten stuck in, and he understood that there had been a breach of the agreement.

The Seer awoke with a terrible anxiety. If the agreements were broken, then what would become of those in the herd who fell? What would become of those who gave themselves to metal jaws or to young boys' arrows or to the medicines of virgin healers? What would become of the gifts from the feathered angels?

He did not ask, in his innocence, what would become of us, we who relied for our growth and our survival on being the recipients of the agreement. It did not occur to him that we could be abandoned by the world; that the medicine would leave. Nor did it occur to him, just yet, to ask why.

One dies a million deaths in the course of one life. In one death, one can also live a million lives. The man lies face up in the snow, dying. The ice is a fine amplifier. In each of its crystals, the man hears the echoes of his pain: Why did I fall? For what? What did I do wrong? Why am I dying? Why does it hurt so much? What didn't I see? What could I have done differently? What could I have known? He tries to move his fingers, but nothing moves. He does not know why he has fallen. He stares at the sky, as though it might answer him. He does not know why no one comes to help him. He does not know why the cold makes the blood rush in his veins and then stills them so that his heart cannot move.

He did not ask what he could have learned. He asked what he could have known. And those, it must be noted, may be—in the course of human lives—two antithetical endeavors.

As his blood settled in his veins and his heart made one last attempt to contract, he vowed he would come back to understand how the ice can still a body so severely that the body can no longer house a soul.

The sun beat down on the plain. They ran as fast as they could. They fed on one another's fear and the sun ran through the follicles of their hair like blinding lightning, confusing them. The pounding of footfalls they did not recognize drove them on like warrior drums. Some of them fell, and as an alchemy so sophisticated that only machines could make it penetrate their hearts or puncture their skulls, they wondered why they fell. They abandoned their bodies in heaps on the plain, not understanding what would become of them or what they had done wrong.

Enormous creatures walked with felted paws over the snow, leaving deceptive impressions of their weight. They hunched their backs against the strength of trees and sniffed the air for caves in which they could feel the cycles of the earth in peace. On their ways, some of them fell, in disbelief and confusion that the forest would've created for them metal mouths that belonged to no one. To die in the heat of the wolf pack's organized frenzy, to be savored by their strength, that was one thing. To die in a mouth of no-creature, to feel nothing but cold linked to no-life, to be stopped mid run by teeth that belonged to no jaw, no blood, no heart, made them cry out to the snakes, the eagles, and the wolves, waiting for an answer. But no one answered them, not while they were alive.

Others lived high above them, armed with senses so sharp that the thick and complicated earth appeared to them as an intricately embroidered veil, and neither distance nor time were a boundary to the sights they could see and the smells they could smell. They swooped down, when the confusion had left the hoofed and footed ones, to try to reengage the agreement. With their slick but weak beaks, they plucked out the eyes in which confusion had settled like mud in a pond. They swallowed. They pulled away the skin from the fat in which the last moments of bewilderment had gathered and had begun to grow sour. They swallowed the fetid stink bit by bit to reveal the sinews in which the fear pooled like blood. They pulled each sinew away, sharing the task among the beetles, the ants, and others of their kind until all that was left were the golden bones, available now, to feel the sun. For that was the way, and that was the agreement.

Only one man prayed. But he did not pray in gratitude. Nor in awe. He prayed as the owner of those bones had died, in confusion and anxiety. The few remnants left of those who fell were trapped or borrowed from he honored in a way the living can only hope for. He arranged the bones of a great grizzly under the sun, cleaned the skull, and caressed the great nails that had once sliced fish from the water. He felt nothing but their hard, sharp scrape against his own hands. He wondered at their strength. He wondered at what this creature had seen, had felt. He fitted the massive structure to his own crown. He carefully pulled it down over his hair and adjusted the angle of it so that his own eyes looked out through the sockets.

That night, he dreamed the strangest dream: A man was born into the world not looking, not seeing, not feeling, but poking, prodding, waiting, as though in revenge against a crime he could no longer remember. Instead of seeing with his hands, hearing with his heart, and breathing with the stars, he carried instruments and theories and experiments to teach him how the world worked. He wrote papers. He came to understand thermostasis in mammals—much to the chagrin of many rats, mice and cats in his lab who spent their lives wondering why the white around them was never cold and why the light did not love them, and who died under his hand feeling the same strange abandonment and confusion that had prompted his return. He began to put the world together according to his own questions, according to the answers he could find, according to the paths he could see, and so the agreements that he could not see—and was no longer looking for—began to come undone, and the whirlwinds of the tornadoes began to slow, and the particles that make up life began to fall out of the vortex, out of love with the movement.

The more they fell, the less the winds of the tornadoes blew, the more anxious the man became about tying the world together according to his perceptions, his reason, his knowledge: and rightly so, it must be said, for without the movement of the tornadoes, such reasons were the only ties holding the world together anymore. The man, despite his coarse senses, seemed to intuit this. However, it must be noted, he could not create new ties as fast as the old ones were becoming undone. He could never catch up with the universe. By the time he had exhausted himself in the effort to tie that which he could not see was falling apart, most of the particles had settled, most of the tornadoes' winds had died down. As he lay dying in the snow, he could find no reason for it at all. Neither could the snow.

The Seer awoke, feeling terrified.

One dies a million deaths in the course of one life. In one death, one can also live a million lives. The man lies face up in the snow, dying. He thinks no thoughts, though he feels confused and humbled like a dog scolded for something he did not know he did wrong. He feels the ice particles separate under his weight and his heat. For a moment, he worries that nothing else will ever happen, so he focuses all his concentration on the subtle shifting of the particles of ice below him. Their movements are his only company, his only sense that there is life around him. He concentrates so desperately that he can begin to feel as one flake warms and shifts around his neck, and he can hear the ones behind that one crinkle and adjust to the new space—if he listens gently enough, it almost sounds like a strange kind of laughter. A strange joy. As the cold washes through his blood, stilling his heart, a tiny wind passes over the man, as though the atmosphere were exhaling, or perhaps stroking the man's face. He closes his eyes and goes to sleep for the last time. But sleep and death are two different things. In sleep, one can dream, and so the man feels himself traveling lightly on that gentle breath of wind, across the snow bank and into one dawn in the evening of time. He now holds in his hands the skull of a great grizzly bear, which seems to acquiesce to his fingers, as though it knew it would arrive there, as though it had arranged to be cleaned and held and tilted. The man notices that unlike most skulls—which look angry or vicious—this one looks peaceful and wise, like a father letting his son win a chess game. He does not know why, but as he traces the smooth forehead of the skull, he feels compelled to put it on his own head. He carefully pulls it down over his hair and adjusts the angle of it so that his own eyes look out through the sockets: he sees the sun beating down on the plain. The horses and gazelles and bison run as fast as they can. They feed on one another's energy and the sun runs through the follicles of their hairs like messages down telephone wire. The pounding of their hooves against the dry ground drives them on like warrior drums. But some of them fall anyway, for that is the way, and that was the agreement.

Others live high above them, armed with senses so sharp that the thick and complicated earth appears to them as a beautifully woven and transparent web, and neither distance nor time are a boundary to the sounds they can hear and the sights they can see.

On the snow bank, a man lies face up, dying. For that is the way, and that is the agreement. His blood, upon registering that he is dying, runs through his veins faster than ever—not to save him, not to protect his organs, but to scavenge the heat left from the fission of soul and body—for there is an agreement, too, between this man's blood and something else in the world. The particles of ice closest to his skin accept the heat and obediently trickle around the man like fawning geisha. The trickle of water expertly scales down the crevices in the ice. As it reaches its apparent destination, it releases the last bit of its heat into a minuscule thread of ice-algae, freeing a tiny krill who has gotten somehow stuck at the bottom of the ice shelf. The baby whale, who is just then opening his great feathered mouth to learn to feed, is rewarded by his first taste of krill.

The Seer awoke, awed and confused by the dream, and in particular, by the last moment of the dream. Of course the blood was not an intentional creature, and the water felt nothing akin to compassion or will, and the man never knew of the baby whale his death was to welcome into the habits of the living. But it was still something. "Perhaps," thought the Seer when he awoke, "there are agreements even between blood and water, between ice and krill. Perhaps one does not have to be grand and large to be part of the agreement, one has to be very small, so small, and so pure, that one can move through the world almost invisible. Perhaps that is the making of love."

One Message

The raindrops patter on the Basho leaf, but these are not tears of grief;
this is only the anguish of him who is listening to them.

Zen saying

An old man whose face has so many
wrinkles that one could get lost in them, or mistake them for the ocean
beds, or for the tracks of wandering souls, waits for an eagle to tell him it
is time.

The girl was very young, perhaps too young to be out in the woods
by herself at night, but she was there anyway because the darkness had
invited her, as though she were going to whisper a special secret to the
girl. While the girl knelt at the edge of the first line of trees, waiting for
the trees to translate the secrets of the darkness, the great horned owl
came to her. He is grand, it is true. But he does not have to maintain airs
the way hawks and eagles do. And so he flew down in front of the girl,
feigned injury to his leg, and waited. Indeed, the girl gasped, reached out
to him, sure he would not come, but he did. He hobbled to her, tucked
his sharp, yet demurely curved, beak into her hand, and closed his eyes.
"Oh my," thought the girl. "What could be wrong? You mustn't die here,
not on me, not now. I would not know what to do! I do not know what to
do to help you!" She felt the hard slick of his beak against the flesh of her
palm and she felt the heat of his closed eyelids.

"Creature," she asked, "why do you come to me?"

The great horned owl first raised his ear tufts, and then his black lids,
revealing shockingly golden eyes. He looked up at the girl, "Because,"

129

he said, betraying his kind, "because I am a messenger and yet those who want the messages do not know what to do with them. Because the messages, once one sees them, are hard to understand, and perhaps—for those to whom they are directed—impossible to bear." He blinked his bright eyes and continued: "Have you seen my kind fly?"

"Yes," said the girl. "The curve of your wings carves through currents that others do not see. And," she added, "it is beautiful."

"I thought I was great, you know," the owl continued, nestling his broad back-feathers against her sweet palms, "the breath of heaven herself. I thought I had the lock that fit the key. I thought the beating of my wings would guide the lost. I flew with the conviction that my feathers would filter the truth from the wind."

"And?" asked the girl, trying so hard to listen to him, for surely owls do not speak often, but oh! the delight of him wanting her to touch him, the trust that felt like the earth herself were welcoming her made her ears fill with her heart and so she had to remind herself to listen and to speak.

"And does it not?" the girl tried again.

"No," he confided, "it often does not."

"And why is that?" asked the girl, still loose from the special warmth that emanated from the wild of the creature as he spoke his heart.

"Most seek answers because they are afraid of missing the truth, and they are afraid of missing the truth because they are afraid they will make the wrong choice, and they are afraid of making the wrong choice because they do not see that the right choice is not right because of them—though they may facilitate it—it is right because in the syncopation of fact, time, and interpretation, it creates harmony in the Five Worlds. They are driven by what they fear they are not, and not driven by what they already are, and therefore, never see where to go. In short, they seek because they want to be found, and not because they recognize that they have been already.

"If I could tell you what would happen in a point of time in the future, what would you know?"

The girl thought for a minute. Knowing the future is supposed to be a powerful thing. One could protect, one could warn, one could know what is going to happen!

"And why," the owl continued, "the eagle would ask—if he were here—'would you want to know what will happen? To stave off fear? To change what should happen? To guard against pain perhaps?' But that is not what the messages are there for, and so I, as a messenger, become distraught. There is only one truth, and there is only one message, and there are a million feathers by which to get there. For some, it takes just one, for others, it takes hundreds of millions of birds. But that is okay, we know how to fly." With that, the great horned owl no longer had to feign injury; he packed his messages into his heart, on which the blood choked itself, and he fell limp in the girl's hands.

The girl walked home from the forest in a terrible hurricane of bewilderment, carrying the dead owl as though there were someplace special she must put him. "Where did he go?" she wondered. "No angels came down to fly him to heaven. The earth did not claim him yet. So where is he?" She reached her front door—her pleasure at having been visited by an owl was now drenched in the feeling she had failed him, and her heart was as limp as his body in her hands.

"Mama," she asked as she entered the kitchen, "why did the owl die?"

"To bring you a message, my child," she said, because that is what she had been told. She wrung her dishcloth tightly because, although she believed what she had been told, she was not sure why she believed it. "That was the agreement the elders had said the ancestors had been the recipients of."

For eons the messengers diligently and enthusiastically make their way to us. They do not stop when we do not understand. They do not resent us. They simply keep going, tireless nannies to our souls and to the worlds they love.

"Mama, is there really a purgatory?" she asked, for if the owl was neither above nor below, then where was he? She had heard such a thing whispered about, and the lights that came out of the darkness made her wonder if it were true, made her wonder about her world.

"What, my child, would that be?" said her mother, aware that the child was asking questions for which she could offer only desiccated platitudes.

"A place," the young child continued, "between heaven and hell?"

"Yes, my child, there is," the mother said, and immediately wondered if she should not have.

"And what, Mama, do the souls do there?" The girl was persistent.

"Well, for a long time, they pretend that they do not know they are in purgatory."

"And when they realize it, Mama, what do they do?"

"Well, some of them sing. Some of them write. Some of them dream.

Some of them feel, and some of them see. Some of them sit in silence, waiting."

"And those who sing? What do they sing about?"

The mother paused for a moment, and then she said, "They sing about what the bird songs do not reveal to them."

"And those who write, what do they write about?"

The mother paused again, and then she said, "My child, I do not know. Perhaps it is less what they write about and more that they try to put down the words in new order, to map the world in a new way, hoping to find the treasure, the heaven's gate. Or, perhaps they chase words like starving wolves chase emaciated rabbits," she paused, "because they are desperate and there is nothing else in their purgatory that will sustain them."

"And those who dream, what do they dream about?"

"The lost worlds—either above or below. They dream about either what is here that isn't seen or about what isn't here but could be. They dream about what isn't said, in ways it isn't said, so that they can then say it. They dream for the same reason I boil water before I give it to you to drink; to clarify their being."

"And those who see, what do they see?" The young girl was relentless.

The mother, tired now, and out of answers said, "I do not know what they see . . . Perhaps there are others in purgatory who wonder that. Perhaps there are some who know that."

"And those who wait, what do they wait for?"

"Oh, my child, they wait for things I no longer believe in—the answer? At least an echo? Perhaps they wait in the hopes that the question will eventually go away."

"Mother," the child said earnestly, "I do not want to be in purgatory."

"I know, child," the mother said. "If you can find the way out, I will be right behind you."

The child dragged the grand—but now limp—owl through the hallway to the living room, where her father sat staring at the fire. When the child asked her father why the owl died, all he said was: "Perhaps because that was the only passage from where he was to where you are."

This does not comfort the girl. She wonders why she is the one in whose hands he died rather than the one in whose hands he was healed. Surely, she thinks, he was sick?

For this, this sort of question, is one of hitches of the zipper between

Here and There, between the agreement and those who are to honor it, between remedy and poison, heaven and hell, healing and damning, past, present, truth and illusion.

By human count, many years after the great horned owl died in the hands of the young girl (who is now becoming a young Portal), she wakes in the mornings feeling as though the wind is waiting for her, that the sun has something to give her, that the shadows are envelopes that contain secrets she should discover, and that even though the birds are clearly calling to one another, she must pay attention because the spirits might have placed an encoded message for her in their calls. She wakes each morning with an anxiety that she does not know what she needs to know. In her dreams, she hears sounds she cannot understand, sees images she cannot remember, and feels sensations she cannot parse. When she wakes, she believes that in some hills, hidden in some valleys, protected by certain trees, there are voices still—not of magic, not of the supernatural, but of what we think we are looking for, what the shadows keep secret. The few who remain to speak, she thinks, they have come so far—across bridges that no longer exist, across climates few could survive, through history and time that was foreignly wild and shockingly violent. They are stranded here now and when they stop speaking, we will be stranded as well. The young Portal is worried that they might stop speaking, or that they might stop speaking before she can hear them. In her most destitute moments, while the mourning doves call back and forth above her head like older children playing ball out of her reach, she wonders if the voices would ever speak to her.

A young boy is left alone for too long: His parents have much to do and he has too little to do. So, the old man—whose face does indeed record not just the tides of the oceans, but also the tracks of many souls and who is biding his time waiting for the eagle—comes to the boy, who has no wonders about the tides of oceans or the tracks of souls, and teaches the boy, in the afternoons, how to make his own bow and arrows.

The girl walks the world anxiously looking. She follows the flutter of each winged creature as it passes her—but each one seems to disappear behind leaves and over hills without ever telling her a thing. She sits for hours in the forest, until her feet can track the digging of the moles below the ground and her ears resound with the percussion of tiny legs over leaves and the scratch of billions of setae over bark. It is all beautiful, but, still, she walks away not knowing what the leaves mean, what the patterns of the earth are for, whose heart the percussive insects conduct, or who feel the tickle of the setae.

In the early dawn of the afternoon in which the cardinals were to war over a particularly fine branch, the young Portal was out walking, unable to stop herself from wondering if somewhere in the flight patterns of the finches, there was a map home. Perhaps it was in the blankets of sound the crickets shook through the air? As she rode the swoops and dips of the crickets' symphonies, she heard the crackle of a fire deep in the woods, in the circle where the elders sat—perhaps conversing with the voices from the hills, perhaps just listening to them. The elders in her village had always seemed so calm. They always smiled as though they were in search of only what happened to present itself, and their eyes focused on whatever happened to present itself as though they were observing a faraway image from a train window or from the back of a speeding horse. What did they know that comforted them so? How did they know who to touch and with what?

It was not like that for the girl. Rather, she felt the world like a powerful ocean around her: some things to walk towards, or into, some things to leave, some things to touch, some things to smell, some things to feel, and the world changed around her, with a mind of its own that would dictate her experience: Some things moved towards her or away, a smell came or went, a spider allowed her to touch it or not, an owl came to her to die in her hands, or not. She felt at its mercy, not as though she were a mere observer.

The Seers, the young Portal knew, parse the world for us—for our use—into "those who know" and "those who do not," into "those on the path" and "those who have lost their ways," into "those who see" and "those who do not," into "those who are sincere" and "those who are not"—all seekers know those tests. But, she was beginning to suspect that the Seers do not want us to take them too literally; or rather, that they were defining the boundaries of purgatory. She was beginning to worry that those who accept these divisions have already defined where they are along the continuum, have already gilded the bars of their cages, have already set the limits to what they are willing to see, have already signed into purgatory. As she stood by the forest, listening, guarded from the circle of wisdom by the trees who shelter by never moving, she wondered if such divisions, tests, and qualifiers were for the unseeing. For the afraid. If they were useful only for those who are still waiting for the world to love them, for the gods to single them out like needles in a haystack. "Do the gods single us out? Is that how it works?" she wondered. "Or perhaps there are special places, places that would transport one from here to another world, to a greater understanding? One simply has to find them. One needs a map? A compass? Is that how it works?"

On this afternoon—the afternoon that the girl was to be in the path of the sun's glint—while she walked and wondered, while the cardinals warred over a prime place on a branch, the boy, who had been working with an old man for many weeks now, had just completed his first well-strung bow.

The young Portal turned the corner to head home. As she walked, she was thinking of the carriers of the medicine, of the messages, of eagles, of hawks, of creatures whom the ancestors had honored. She was thinking of the home she had always sensed was there and could never smell. She thought of the beautiful young man she had known the summer before—well, not just known, listened to, dove into. He spoke in verse and sung phrases from those who knew the whole song—from those who lived on the other sides of purgatory. He said things like, "Don't look down: the path will disappear; Let's go into the forest and see what the trees have to say!; We can go have a picnic and watch the sounds of the water—but bring your own sun. I will pull the clouds over us for shade." And, on the occasion they crossed a snake, he said: "Never be afraid of nature unless she is afraid of you. Never make nature afraid." But the boy, it seemed, had looked down. He had left her, and with no sun of her own, no clouds, no path she could see, and no water she could hear. The trees did not say anything, as far as the young Portal could tell. Snakes still startled her. He had gotten bored, perhaps, or perhaps he spoke like a parrot, repeating phrases from the voices in the hills but never able to link them into a coherent reality. In any case, he seemed to the young Portal just one more promising envelope that turned out to be empty.

As she walked the dirt road, the dust half-heartedly flirted with the roots of the short weeds and the needles of the prickly pines. The striped lizard's erratic scampers caught her eye. The fat robin stood idle in the grass. Three male cardinals warred over a crescent joint on the great oak tree, and a pileated woodpecker kept his own time and did not bother to heed the dancing of the bees. A vulture traced spirals in the sky around— it seemed to the young Portal—her. From a distance, they look big and majestic like the revered birds. But up close, she thought, they were kind of grotesque. Not only that, but they did not even really hunt! All that size and grandeur to merely pick decay caused by a power greater than they had.

"I wonder," thought the girl, "why do so many eagles and hawks come to the elders, come to others, but not to me? I am circled by a vulture.

"Surely I am lost, and I am stuck in purgatory. And who needs a messenger more than one who is lost or stuck? Perhaps I am not sacred enough?"

A red-bellied woodpecker's call rang out unanswered just then, for her mate's beak was full of grub he was bringing back to the brood.

The young Portal was, at this moment, being watched by the elders who sat in the woods around the last embers of the night's fire. They had watched her before, when she had carried home a dead owl, when she had dived into the boy out of whose mouth phrases from the voices in the hills fell like surprise rain showers, as she envied the way the snakes ignored him and the eagles came to him—allowing him to stroke their feathers as though they were runes—as she wondered, with a pang in her gut, what secrets the sacred creatures were telling him. Wondering if they were telling him the way out, the way to hold owls without their dying, the way not to be in-between.

They watched her watch the buzzards. They watched her shake her head and allow disappointment to kill off a tiny part of her heart.

They watched her walk with her mind focused on what she feared she did not know, and they watched her miss what was right in front of her. It is true, they do not watch everyone. So why were they watching this young girl?

They might answer like this: It is not that some are special and others are not. It is not that some are in particular need and others are not. We scream to the gods because we believe no one else can take the deafening volume of our minds, not because the gods demand it, or even hear our desperation if it increases in decibel. It is simply that the tracks of some lives run along the seam between worlds and those tracks are observed and taken care of by the gods, for those tracks are like zippers and can be closed or opened by each step the life on them takes—when they open, bits of heaven can travel to us. And the gods want heaven to reach us. That is how they breathe—but how it does so is as much a mystery to them as it is to us. Sometimes, heaven can reach us directly, and other times, it must come through those who have come before us, the ancestors some call them, the voices in the hills others call them, who seem locked from our immediate access to them by moats of time or ravines of misinformation and blindness.

This girl's life was on such a track. And she felt, as most of the Portals do, that there was some bridge her mind or her heart must cross; that there was something she must know, some guidance she should have, some sacredness bestowed upon her that would validate her sense that her life was more than her own, that her ache to know more or to see more was divine and not neurotic. She looked for the sacred. She waited for the angel's feathers, she looked between the particles of sunlight, waiting for the great eagle or the great tortoise, or the great snake to come to her and give her direction. But the sacred did not come to her. The eagles flew over someone else, dropped their feathers for someone else. The owls perched at the windows of other people's homes now, lived—and perhaps died—for other little girls. The snakes protected the young boy, not her. This is what she saw. And each time she looked and did not see, each time she heard an eagle's call that was not for her, her mind told her heart that there was nothing special to see. There was nothing missed, not for her anyway—and so sealed one tooth of the zipper closed.

On this day, the day the cardinals warred over a particularly prime tree branch, the elders decided it was time to begin helping the girl—lest the track become sticky with the black tar of the blindness of those who are supposed to see.

For we may think that if we do not see where we are supposed to that that is our personal loss, but it is not so. When eyes that are supposed to see are closed, the heart to whom they belong cries thick black tears through which all future travelers of that track must pull themselves, and which make the gates between Here and There hard to open and close.

The Maiden of the Elders (so-called because she looked much younger than the others of the group, even though she had swum across the moats and scaled the ravines between this world and another so many times that they now disappeared in deference upon her arrival) decided to place herself on the last turn of the dirt road, about a mile and a half from where the girl would find her first eagle.

On this day also, the young boy walked, carrying his new bow to the edge of the woods that guarded his property. He gazed into the sky ornamented with leaves and looked carefully for any signs of life. The old man who had taught him had made only one condition: Never shoot at anything. The boy listened, smelled, and watched the sky and, seeing nothing, he drew back the braided guts of the buffalo, the ash backbone stilling itself against the tension between Here and There. The emptiness of the sky beckoned him to release the quiver into it. And so he did. He watched it arc over the leaves, past where he could see. The boy was pleased. He smiled. His bow worked! His arrow shot straight! The old man would be very proud, he thought.

The Maiden of the Elders brought with her to the last turn of the dirt road a basket woven of prairie grasses in which she would put the herbs for which she would be foraging when the girl rounded the bend. She went to the center of the field, looked to the sky, and saw the forebreath of a great black eagle trace its entrance in the sky. It took about 5 minutes before the bird actually arrived, piercing the wind he was accustomed to riding, propelled by a joy that must release itself in earsplitting screams. His aim was flawless: Hitting the random arrow shot from a boy's homemade bow exactly in the major artery of his great black neck. As he then free-fell through wind that had been his earth, feeling an ecstasy rare for birds of any sort—feeling what it feels like for us when we imagine flying—he released one final trill of joy and hit the grassy field on his left shoulder, skidding to a stop just at the feet of the Maiden of the Elders. He turned his obsidian eyes to the woman, blinked once as his wing folded into him for the last time, felt the earth gathering beneath him to carry him to his next destination, and relaxed his great muscles. The Maiden of the Elders smiled down at him, awed still—after all this time—at the dedication of the messengers, at their joy and their trust. She bent down, plucked one large flight feather from his folded wing, stroked his back, straightened his neck, and walked to the lush bushes where the young Portal would be rounding the corner any minute. She smiled as she tucked the eagle's feather into the top of her long braid. "If that does not attract her, I don't know what will," she thought.

The girl walked past the cardinals cutting invisible divisions in the air, past the pileated woodpeckers, past the stillness of the trees that guarded the way. As she rounded the bend she caught sight of an ancient-looking woman who appeared to be so deep in her work that she did not turn to see who made footfalls on the nearby road. The girl stood and watched. The woman moved so slowly, touching one leaf and then another, as though waiting for the plants to tell her which to pick and which to avoid. Atop her head a beautiful feather stood like a sentinel.

The young Portal, on impulse, said quietly, "Excuse me." The ancient woman did not alter her rhythm. The young girl stepped closer. "Excuse me. May I ask you a question?" The woman turned towards the girl, still stooped over the lavender she was about to harvest.

"I am sorry to interrupt you. Can you tell me how you know which plants to pick and which to leave? Which are the medicines and which are the poisons?"

The woman looked at the young girl and said, "Well, first of all, there is no difference between medicine and poison. There is only the use of the correct thing for the correct thing. Anything can be medicine and anything can be poison."

"And how do you know what to use for what, then? How do you know how to keep things like medicine and not like poison?"

The old woman thought for a moment, and in a bit of a gamble, said, "The messengers."

The girl's heart leapt and pulled itself down at the same instant. "I have been waiting for the messengers for a long time," said the girl. "Why do they come to some of us and not to others?"

The ancient woman remained stooped over the lavender and smiled slightly. "You have been waiting for the messengers?" she asked, as though repeating the location someone was asking directions to.

"Yes!" said the young Portal. "I have seen them come to others. I have an opening in my soul, or between my soul and myself in which I await the directions. I want to be warned by the snake not to enter the brush, or to be told by the owls that tomorrow will bring dangers. I want the wolves to tell me how to lead, if I am to lead. I want, when someone is ailing, or sad to know which herb will heal them and which words will correct them." The young woman paused, eager to say so much and worried that she would say too much. "I want to see the messages. I want them to come to me." She stopped herself then, for she saw the ancient woman's eyes scanning a world millennia away. The lavender bush below the ancient woman brushed eight of its sprigs against her hand and lay patiently in her palms until she plucked them. "Child," she said, "what makes you think the messengers do not come to you?"

The young girl thought. It seemed so clear in her mind before she had been asked the question. The resentment, the frustration, the slight mold of jealousy, the disappointment that greeted her each day. But more than that, it was as though everywhere she went to look seemed empty and such emptiness over the course of years begins to feel damning, as though the world were rejecting her.

"Because I feel lost," she finally said. "And alone. Because if they come, I do not see them, and I do not know what they say. And," she said, "because one of them died in my hands a long time ago. It should have lived. I should have known the medicine to help it."

"Ah," said the ancient woman. "Well, perhaps that is just a matter of time. Time can do that . . . can stretch us out across the world so that it seems as though none of our footfalls takes us anywhere. But if you just move through it, you come to see that it is just a superficial film. And you may find, that because of it, you must separate your understanding of the messages from the space and time of their coming. The black and white feathers of the woodpecker fall in a different place from his red crown feathers when he is taken by the eagle."

The young woman listened, but she did not understand. So the ancient woman continued:

"If the eagle plucks a rare woodpecker from the wind, some feathers falling here, and others there, then what thing is the message? Who is the messenger? The eagle? The first clutch of feathers she plucked from the woodpecker—which happened to land on your path? Or, is it rather, the majestic red head that she severed with one twist of her great beak, which landed miles away on an abandoned railroad where no human will ever find it? Is it the rare bird who died to give his feathers to you and to the iron rods of a railroad? Who is to say that the eagle is not simply catching her dinner? Who is to say that an old woodpecker does not care if he is rare, for it was his time to go and he wanted to go on the wings of a warrior? If a needle shines in a haystack, that is because it is already in the light's path, not because the light seeks it, my child. The light shines on everything that is available to it. Do you hear the trees?"

The girl listened, but all she heard was the rustling of crows in the leaves. "No, I am afraid I do not. I was told, once before, though that they speak. I have never heard them, and I cannot hear them now."

"They speak. Perhaps you will hear them through me . . . The trees, they find that stillness helps them grow towards the heavens. Stillness makes them tall; time comes to them. That is their choice. To let time come to them while they are still so that they can reach towards below the earth and above towards the heavens. But, if it is your choice, you can move and let time stand still. Time is merely the distance we put between ourselves and the things we do not understand. Oddly, the more of it we create, the longer it takes us to understand."

The girl felt a sudden urgency, as though she were late for something. "Thank you. I don't know what else to say and I must get home."

"Of course you must, my dear. Go on. Walk as though the ground were a canvas on which all the paintings of the world have already been painted. See what you see. The messengers paint the truth over and over. They do not tire, even though it can take us so long to understand. The question is"—the ancient woman could not help herself because the truth is giddy-making, even to an immortal—"Why do they not tire of us? Why do the messengers not tire? Answer that question and you will receive the messages."

At that moment, around the other side of the great forest, a young boy ran looking for an old man, whose face did indeed record the tides of oceans and the travels of souls, to tell him that his arrow had shot clean. The boy walked deep into the forest, deeper than he'd ever been until he came across a simple fire pit, around which old beggars sat, boiling tea. He asked them, "Have you seen a very old man, one who can make his own bows and arrows?" The old folks smiled. "Yes, dear boy. We have seen him, but he has gone on now. He has swum the moats and climbed the ravines and is now talking in the hills with voices you and I can no longer hear." The boy looked puzzled and a little frightened. So, the old folks asked, "Did your arrow shoot straight?"

"Yes!" said the boy.

"Did it fly far?"

"Yes!" said the boy.

"Did you aim it at anything?"

"No, no!" said the boy. "Only open sky. The old man said never to aim it at any living creature."

"Well then," the old folks continued, "it must have crossed over the moats, flown the ravines, and that means he can see it! In fact, it likely landed right at his feet. He must be very proud of you."

The boy smiled, for that was all he wanted, really. The Maiden of the Elders heard him walk calmly back towards his home, his mind content and undisturbed by the mysterious words he'd heard from the other elders, and so she resumed grooming the lavender for tea.

The young Portal walked on towards home, too, wondering what that graceful ancient woman could've meant. Before she had taken eight steps, she saw large feathers protruding awkwardly from the grasses and she saw the inelegant hop and bobble of a buzzard as he plunged into the breast meat of what appeared to be a black eagle. She grimaced a bit at what she took to be the disrespect of a great warrior by a mere scavenger, but she walked towards the scene anyway.

Perhaps, she thought grimly, the messages for me are not so grand. I do not get hawks that land on my arm, nor butterflies on my toes, nor do I get the calls of eagles while I am running: perhaps for me, I get the eagle after he has landed. After he has ridden the wind, after his greatness has turned into something the common buzzard and maggot flies can digest. "Okay," she thought, turning towards the vultures, "then I am one of you. Perhaps you also have a way out of here." She crouched by the fallen eagle, brushed off flies, suffered bites on her toes by red ants. She followed the buzzards in debriding the eagle of what he no longer had use for. She took five flight feathers from the eagle and looked around at her company. She felt from them an odd sincerity—even a serenity. "Take care of him," she said to them, "I do not know how." With that, the buzzards bobbed their heads as if in agreement and finished purifying the eagle of that which had kept him in that world.

Every night for many years, the Portal stroked her black feathers, wondering what their special powers were, what those who knew their sacredness would see in them. In the ocean of her world many tides came and went. The girl walked endlessly, through ravines, up mountains, searching still for the ones who speak the harmony through which the Five Worlds converge, the ones who could teach her how to be seen by the sun. As she walked, trees bent to her, snakes slithered in her path, ravens called to her, cardinals made conversation, wolves recited the moon's poetry from around bends in mountains, the winds tickled her mind—she saw now, that every sway of this great body of water was trying to tell her something, but still, she did not know what it said.

Noting that the girl's persistence was of the same quality as that of the tireless messengers, the High Priest, the one who watches over the gates between the worlds, decided it was finally time for the girl to find him. He set his cave atop a mountain she would climb, prepared the fire, and he waited. After her lifetime of questions to others along the way, she found herself on the dirt floor of his cave, her hands dusted with the dander of a mountain who does not need to know that the rain is essential to it remaining a mountain, and said: "Master, I see the messengers. They come to me. They come fast and furious sometimes. One after another as though there is some urgent message I am to get. At the beginning of my life, I waited for the messengers to come. And now that they come, I do not understand the message."

The High Priest blew on the small, perfect stones in the fire pit, walked to the eave of the cave, looked out over the fir-dressed cliff, turned towards the young Portal and said, "The beating of wings and the calls from beaks shaped to bridge the divide between this world and another come. But to whom? For what?"

The young Portal was confused. "Yes," she said, patting the clay from her palms, "to me, but for what?"

The High Priest neither smiled nor grimaced. He folded his black canvas dress neatly around his calves as he knelt by the modest fire.

"Why?" is all he said.

"Why?" thought the Portal, "'Why?' The logic is off here. I did not ask . . . I do not know what I did not ask, but I am certain that his question circumvents mine." At that moment, she felt very small, very opaque, very ill-equipped. She felt as though she had gotten nowhere, accomplished nothing. Found no one. All of that life aimed to find the interpreter, the master, the High Priest in the hills who would help the gods spot her as the sun's brilliance glinted off her edges deep in the piles of hay.

The High Priest blew again on the fire, for the Portal's confusion had dampened the coals. He waited as the stones received the very heat they generated and glowed in pride.

"Do you mean," she said, "why do they speak to me? As though perhaps I am wrong? Perhaps they should not?" The sun blinked just then and the young Portal felt her metal go dull as the dry grass.

But that is not why the sun blinked.

The clouds loosened their clasped hands and rain began to release its sounds against the grey rocks, against the soft feathers of the nested whip-poor-wills, against the bounce of the pine needles, and into the communion of the river below.

The High Priest waited till the mountain clay silently accepted the drops of rain and then he said to the young Portal, "The gods speak endlessly! The fall of the raindrops is their language; there is no need for the intermediary of a master, nor of a messenger—one only has to understand the rain. Do you understand the rain?"

The Portal did not. She sat by the rocks whose purpose was to receive and transmit the fire that would destroy them. She listened to the rain, but just as the majestic stripes of the great horned owl drew her attention, but did not reveal any great truth, and just as the vibrations of the eagle feathers in her hair made her alert, but she did not know to what, and just as the crossing of the turtle made her aware, but she did not know to what she should attend, she heard the rain, but she did not understand the rain.

The High Priest sat. "That is okay," he said. "Wait. Perhaps there is a messenger who will come and who will teach you about the message. For where we are, there is only one message. There was a time, or a place—depending on which gem you peer through—in which, it seems from here, there were lots of different 'messages.' But really, it was not so; it was just that we walked in the world—then or there—not on the other side of it, and so the elements and movers of the world spoke to us as they speak to each other. Now, there is one message. Many tireless messengers, but only one message." And so the young Portal sat, listening to the rain that she did not understand. In the meanwhile, she thought over the life that brought her there, the faith that messages meant something. She tried to hold off the thought that it had all been a ruse, that her needle had no sheen, that the gods would never find her because the sun must blink, and the sun must sleep . . . and perhaps she was just one of the many needles who would never be found. Yes, she tried to focus on the sounds of the rain she did not understand, on the calmness of the master in front of her, and on the path by which she had arrived at his fire pit. She thought of all the masters she had been given. She remembered the first eagle she found, the owl who came to her only to die in her hands, but she still did not understand.

After a while, the rain subsided. The High Priest blew again on the coals. The Portal felt a slight tickle on her hand. Looking down, she saw a small black fly walking across her knuckles as though walking over precarious ice.

The High Priest spoke then: "It is an odd act of faith," he said, looking at the fly, "for a soul to let part of itself become a body. Even so light a body as a fly." He nudged the coals with his stick, and sat down again.

The Portal felt that the fly should escape, back out of the cave, into the open sky. But she did not move.

"The fly," the High Priest said, "is humble, but persistent. It will flee instead of fight, but it usually returns for whatever it came for. It means to be only itself. It is an honest creature, but it will take as much as it can. Never more, though. It flies, it grooms its legs and wings. It mates. It is usually completely preoccupied with its primary role of leaving invisible maps in the wind for the special scavengers who can see them—that is part of its agreement—the vultures cannot only see farther and more accurately than we, but they can see things we could never see, no matter how close to them we are. The flies do not know this, but they leave maps anyway. Sometimes, however, the fly takes a break from its work and looks at us, cocking its compounded eyes this way and that. It can be still as death or move faster than the human eye can follow. It can tickle the backs of hands, or walk unnoticed across shoulders. One fly is indistinguishable from another, but they take no notice of that. Go ahead, release him."

With that, the Portal stilled herself, cupped her free hand around the fly and closed it. As she carefully walked to the opening of the cave, she felt the fly scampering up and then down the hills and ravines of her palm. She stood for a moment there—the sun made the residual drops of rain flicker and shine on the leaves like Christmas lights—and then she opened her hands to release the fly.

When she opened her hands, however, there was nothing there. She gasped slightly, and turned to the High Priest with her eyebrows pinched in confusion and concern. "Did I kill him?" asked the Portal, remembering her pain at the owl who had come to her and apparently abandoned her—no, perhaps cursed her—with his death. The priest smiled at her directly, for the first time. "What did you feel towards the fly, child?"

The Portal thought for a moment and then said, "I felt something very light, something very gentle, I just felt as though he needed to be free, to make his maps, to clean the dust from his wings and fly."

"Then," he said, turning back to the coals, "perhaps you, too, are a messenger. And perhaps the fly—in his simplicity and honesty—received the message, perhaps he went to the hills, where the voices still speak the truth, where the ancestors still know the medicines, where the people are able to receive more than one message. So, child, what is the message?"

The Portal walked just outside the cave. She put her hand against the trunk of the quaking aspen, who watched over the cave. Against the tree she felt a vibration, a pulsing, like a strange code, and as she listened, she felt an overwhelming calm, as though she were being watched over by the canopies of every forest. And then came the words, though the Portal did not hear them through her ears, "We find that standing still is our way to reach through earth and up to heaven. We stand still. That is our way and our choice. We let time come to us, let the earth wrap around us as we move through her, and inhale the clouds as we pass through them. This is our way. You can follow us, if you are very very still, if your movement is so slight, so light that it will not disturb even a lichen."

"That we are merely passing through," the Portal finally turned to the High Priest and answered. "That one can pass through and that the paths up and down the ravines and over the moats are coated in a gold so fine that genuine love slides over them so fast there is no distance between here and there—that is why they do not tire of us. The message is eternal and they need travel no distances to bring it to us. Though, perhaps, we must travel distances to reach them."

At that moment, a young man, whose face was sculpted by ocean beds and the tracks of wandering souls, found himself on the side of the world in which there are no moats to cross and no ravines to scale. Wondering if he was alone, he called out and was answered by the haunting trill of a great horned owl. In the grass by his feet, a carefully made arrow still quivered. The man looked down at the ash bow cut by innocent hands; he admired the modest feathers it bore and the meticulous care that had bound them. And he said out loud, "Is that how one gets home? Gets here?" His call was answered by a deep, harmonic echo from the nearby hills.

The Agreement

Nothing in the cry of Cicadas suggests that they are about to die.

Matsuo Bashō

The silence can be horrible for you, we know. But it does not pain us to watch. This is not because we are cruel, and it is not because we do not hear you, and it is not because we do not love you.

The man sits alone listening, or reading or watching, or feeling—it doesn't matter, for he is always alone, and there is no real answer, no matter what he does. He has been asking for eons. He has been a follower of the agreement, a questioner of it, an opponent of it. But when he is alone, and sitting, he is just alone and no one answers. He has learned just to wait.

This image, after a long while, can be endearing. Touching even. For he listens, he watches, he reads. He cannot understand how the earth's dresses caress him in such mesmerizing rhythms: He cannot even see all their folds—but he knows they are there, for he feels the crests and valleys of their movements as though he is riding blindfolded on the ocean. And more than this, he knows there is something that undulates all the more subtly hidden under the folds of fabric. But he does not, not when he is alone and quiet, try to lift the hems. He knows that despite his desire, he cannot be the aggressor. It has taken him many generations to know this. But now he knows. And now, like a matured lover who sees clearly what he wants, he will not let go of it, but he must wait for it to come on its own. He sits, hands folded, face open and soft, eyes charcoaled by the

149

fire that has now become mercury in him—for he will change his shape for the one he loves, if that is what she wants of him. When the silence and the waiting wear on him, and the loneliness overtakes him, he proposes his question. The silence and the waiting wear on him more than he would like, so he proposes over and over.

I can hear you; we can hear you. You have struggled so much to understand. You have shed, mostly, your sense that the world has rejected you, we will now speak directly to you; you are beginning to accept her as she is—she is the one you love, no? So she must be taken as she is. It has taken a long time to understand this. You now can look into a forest and begin to see that the dragonfly takes no notice of you, that the trees stand for themselves—and for the woodpeckers—and not for your use. You no longer resent this. In fact, you are beginning to appreciate it—and it is because of that inchoate shimmer of true joy that your question turns my head—finally. You have to shake your head once or twice to clear your mind, but then you can look and see that the old raccoon under the bushes behind the pines, who is gasping his last breath, is not, in fact, calling for your help—he is simply sharing his final expressions of being alive with all that is living. Do not walk to him. Do not call to him. Do not startle him. Let him feel the company of the living, not the anxiety of those who do not understand life. Good.

Your heart pinches for a moment, I know. That is okay. That is a side effect of being human, a side effect of mistaking compassion for acts that make things live as we would like our lives to be, instead of understanding that compassion is welcoming things to live as they, in fact, should live. It is a residual effect of only being recipients of the agreement, and not part of those in on the agreement. So, I cannot blame you for that. You, like everything else in the world, must be what you are. I smile here. To judge you for that would be a terrible disappointment, a terrible hypocrisy. You would have spent your faith for nothing. So do not worry. I see you. I want you to be as you are. I have waited patiently for you to become what you now are.

So, as I said, I hear your proposal, your plea: "What is the agreement? Why are we not in on it?" you ask.

Well, my dear, because we could not let you in on the secret. We must answer now, for you have polished the dull tarnish off of much of your soul, and the sun glints off of you now—when you are quiet and still. So we will tell it to you now, in the hopes that you will join us. We risk everything in doing so. But the gamble is not ours alone; you risk every-thing as well. Are you ready? Do you really want to be in on the secret? You are eager, that is true. You are patient, when you are alone, at least. You have an incredible energy pulsing behind your modest demeanor, like a young girl about to find her strength. This is how we will think of you. This, perhaps, is how we must think of you.

We all know how the world came to be: it went from wholeness to division and from stillness to movement. We are the result of the Whole shaking, moving, dancing, and coming apart. We live in her veins now, in her cells, in their electrons and neutrons, in the leaves or the branches, or the birds who grip the branches with their talons, which live differently than their feathers. The world came to be because the Whole shimmied. In the spaces between her, now, we too can dance. All the other living things understood this. You were the only creature to believe that cre-ation was the result of union. So, we could not let you in on the secret. You felt apart, and you were in awe, and you assumed that the feeling you have when you come together—not being alone anymore—and the result of that feeling—ownership of a new creature, equaled love and creation. Even when you were humbled and no longer fancied yourself masters of creation, you still clung to the feeling of union as though that were, in fact, creation. When you did not have it, you felt alone and bereft of love. Creation is not, as you believe, the unification of disparate things. That is not creation. Creation is what happens in the space that opens when perfection is divided. And love, love is not something that comes to you, something the living seek or find or lose; it is what makes the living alive.

So what is the agreement? The agreement was to secretly monitor and preserve the union that appeared to have been destroyed. It was to thread webs between all the living creatures, and to vigilantly monitor those threads so that no one thing, not even a particle, fell out of the Whole. The Whole shimmied and divided, that is true, and we exist in the spaces between, but we maintain the integrity of the Whole through our relationships; through the divisions that make relationships possible. The agreement is what ensures that the gods can breathe—the world can expand and contract like lungs. It is an endless and intricate art, sustaining the divisions of creation! One must be capable of complete vigilance—interrupted by nothing, no matter what happens—to carry the secret.

The man listens. He feels. But what he mostly worries about is whether or not he can be so vigilant, whether or not he can carry the secret. Perhaps his vessel is too scarred, too weak, or not weathered enough.

The silence has become a comfort—almost a presence on its own to the woman. The woman sits alone listening, or reading, or watching—it doesn't matter, for she is always alone—and there is no real answer, other than silence. She has been asking for eons. She has been a follower of the agreement, a questioner of it, an opponent of it. But when she is alone, and sitting, she is alone and no one answers. She has learned just to wait. In the quiet, she finds that nothing is still. The wood under her chair shifts imperceptibly and a tiny spider, smaller than a drop of ink, scampers through the cracks in the floorboards. He does not ask where is he going, she notes. He does not wonder what his path is; he does not question his role. He just walks towards the corner of the room, as though there is no other direction in which to walk. When he reaches the corner, he rests in the dust. There is a spiderweb draped between the ceiling and the wall above him. In the web, the weaver thumps her threads, as though checking it for an incoming meal.

The woman watches the web, feels how each thread is an extension of the queen who has created it—like a million limbs, each obeying her but existing on their own. As the woman is lulled by the rhythmic pulsing of the threads, she continues her waiting, and feels a slight envy of the spider's confidence, but she begins to doze off anyway. Her mind follows the spider to the dust in the corner of the room, but she is dozing, and so she does not follow her mind.

To the spider, her mind says, "She has been waiting a long time. She has become very patient. She is endearing now, no? Perhaps it is time to answer her question? She is so very still now! She has rubbed off the dull tarnish of much of her self, and the sun glints off of her, refracting clean waves of joy. Perhaps it is time to tell her the secret?"

The woman is now content that she is sleeping, that she is dreaming. She no longer envies the spider.

In the corner of this room, the spider quietly responds, "I will rest in the dust. The dust will cling to the tiny hairs on my legs. To try to shake the dust, I will walk this wall. But the climb will do little to reduce the dust, for the dust has agreed to help me fulfill my agreement. All of a sudden, I will find that I have reached the weaver's web, up at the top of this climb. The dust will make me sticky and will prevent any attempt to escape I might make. Though I do not know if I will make one. I do not need to know that, and neither does the dust. Once I am in the web, whether I struggle or not, I will have to stay—the dust will ensure that. While I am there, I will see a butterfly wave from the window. He will not be the weaver's dinner today because the weaver will come and make a meal out of me, and then I will be small enough to be carried in the gods' veins. I do not know where the gods will bleed again, or how long it will take for me to emerge through one of their wounds, but eventually, I will emerge again, and walk again the poetry of the secret, and reinforce the threads of our divisions so that creation can breathe—for it can only breathe where it is not."

The woman's mind moved then, to the window, where, indeed a butterfly hovered as though pausing to check the time in a race. "I wear my wings like a geisha her kimono," he said, "mostly, because I feel beauty, but also, to attract your attention. To what? Ah . . . well, that I do not have time to answer. My life is short, and I have blades of grass on which to perch, flowers to make love to, and window frames on which to sit so that I can remember what I was before I looked like this." With that, he flew away, across moats of time and ravines of misinformation and blindness. The woman's mind is awed by the way his waves of beauty part the winds for him. She cannot help but follow him to where he finally stops and rests against the outer wood of a window, on the other side of which, sits a man, waiting, and listening into the silence.

His sadness is so clean and gentle. His hope, she can see, is not a persistent sort that aims for disappointment, but rather, it exists simply to line his patience, as though to protect it. She can hear the thoughts that circle his mind like an endless mantra. He asks, as though proposing to a woman who, he is sure, will eventually say yes: "What is the agreement?"

"I can hear you," she hears herself saying to the man through the window. "I am speaking to you. To you who are listening directly. I can do that because you are not I. But it is to you we speak. And we can speak together, because we are not each other, we are not one. Most of us—I speak for ourselves, not yourselves—do not have to speak to fill the veins that connect the divisions, but we do have to move, to transmit the secret over and over. Across vast distances. Impassable barriers, drowned bridges, infinite faults and crevices, impossible unions—this is the blood flow that keeps the veins alive, that brings nourishment to all of the world's parts, that allows the gods to breathe.

I am not you, you are not me, and in that division, is the union of our creation. Do you see? Do you see how we are now one? I carpet our divide with the textures you are familiar with; will you walk the carpet? Eventually, if you do, you will find me. I am right here, after all."

There is a man, sitting alone, reading this now. He is not you. You are not he. If you can feel what connects you, then you know the secret, you are one of those in on the agreement.

There is a woman, sitting alone, reading this now. You are neither he nor she. If you can feel what connects you, then you are the secret. Welcome to the agreement.

THE
TEMPLE

We do not hear the truth because we are holding out for what we want to hear; we do not see the truth because only what we expect to see appears; we do not feel the truth because we would rather feel what comes to us than wait, and perhaps, feel nothing.

"They" say many things, but they tend to say them over and over in different ways. I have heard most of them, if not all. I have listened for millennia. Men take a long time to change. Listening is hard. Much harder than the ears pretend.

The ears are deceptive: clever and chimerical gatekeepers of how the Way sounds, of what we can hear of it. They are clever in that they appear to be always open; one cannot shut off the ears. Nonetheless, their gates do not swing.

There are many things to see; or rather, "They" show us many things. I have seen many of them—as have many men. But the eyes are even more deceptive than the ears, for they pretend to discern, and their gates open and close, assuring us that when they are open, they see. They are so dogmatic in their certainty about what the mind will take as real—but they must not be trusted. Seeing is nearly impossible with the eyes open.

The truth can be felt; I have felt more than I can understand. The skin and the organs are different from the ears and the eyes. They respond to what they sense honestly, like an animal or a child. They have no trouble telling the mind something is there that cannot be seen, heard or understood, and they do not seem to care if the mind responds. The hairs will rise anyway. The chill or warmth will be registered in the neck, the liver or the kidneys. The heart will contract whether or not one wills it and the truth, or the lie, or the spirits, can tickle one's neck and make one turn one's head even if there is nothing to see or hear. But, despite their honesty, the skin and the organs are loyal to survival of the organism, not to the soul.

I know all of this to be true, but she still waits for me, for me to come back to her. She waits on her heels at the dock, with the waves building and rushing over her. The fact that I know all of this does not stop her from waiting for me and does not stop me from feeling that I cannot reassure her.

"One must walk one's own path; no one can walk it for you." That is one of the things they say, one of the things the ears register.

"There is no distance between now and then and there is no time between here and there." They also say this, and part of that huge truth can squeeze through the Oval Window and reach the half-cocked cochlea.

I have climbed the mountains as they rose over and over in front of me like waves. I know, now, that the summit of each one is the gods' attempt at humor, and I have learned to laugh too. I have leapt over gorges that only I can see and that are a danger only to me. I have sat by the masters in penance for each failed lesson, and while at peace that I was going to learn more, have been ecstatically slaughtered during my meditation. My masters have been wise, have been patient, have been generous; they cleaved me from each life just when I had learned what I could from it and needed to move to the next. They were ruthless with my heart that way, so that it would not pull my soul away from the stars, and of course, so that it would always want more. And they were dedicated. I was not to live each life for its own culmination; no, they made this clear: I was to live each life for the culmination of my soul. Damn the life itself. Damn what is left undone, damn the loves left behind.

As I moved from one life to the next, I looked down, once or twice, despite the fact that they told me not to. I saw the weeping. I felt the bewilderment of those left behind like waves beating against a breaker. I saw her crumpled on the edge of the dock looking out and waiting for me. I know I have left her. I have promises unfulfilled—and not just for her heart, but also for mine. But we all must walk our own paths. That is what They say. They also say that there is no distance in time and no time in distance, and so as I am being pulled away from the sight of her pressing her cheek into her knees to still the terrible pain and confusion, I yell down from the sky, "I am right next to you! There is nothing that separates us! When you can see, feel and hear this, we will be together forever." Of course, forever is now, and then, and one life is separated from the others only as smell is from sight—nothing less and nothing more. But she does not yet see this.

Then They pull me away from my transgression—my melancholy for the distance between here and there and now and then, between she or he and me—and into the great Coral Hall.

The first time, it is a balm, bathing one in the comfort that what They said was true: Here, Lady Wei dances with Lao Tzu, and then with your father. Issa dances with Bashō. Sun Su smiles as she passes by a monk I used to be, before what I am now. The monk does not smile, but his energy reverberates in appreciation. The floor, like the walls and the pillars, are a soft coral, like peach skin stretched over a distant sun. There is a fountain, down which the water makes love to white and coral lights. The dancing never stops, but the music changes, and those who are dancing shift positions. In this place, all dance to the same music. This is where everything comes together, the place where everything turns out okay, turns out correctly. It is created and sustained by the faith of those who cannot see it—each time they override their fear of the unknown and have faith in the way, believing that somewhere, at some time, all will turn out correctly. This is where clouds make the shapes of souls so that the people do not need mirrors. This is where immortals can touch the hands of mortals. This hall is between the arch of the gods' smiles. This is the dance in which all is exactly as it is. There are no lost souls here, there are no mismatches here. All is in balance and harmony.

I have been there, to this great hall. I know it exists. Perhaps it is a kind of heaven. I have danced there. But that does not mean that I am not afraid.

"Master, I am still afraid. I have seen the eternal, danced in the Coral Hall, heard the music which sustains all life and danced to the harmony in which all things are as they should be, but I am still afraid."

"And when do you feel that?" the master asks.

"When I live my own life. Should not this confirmation of the way, of the correctness, of the ultimate harmony help ease my anxiety?"

"Did you see your beloved at the dance?" the master asks me.

I think. I know it felt as though, when I was there, everyone was there, but it is true, I did not see her.

"No," I say. "I did not see her."

"And now?" asks the master. "Do you see her now?"

"The falling stars are what we can see, feel and hear of the rippling of the masters' cloaks when they fly through the heavens. No, I do not see her, now," I say.

"I see," he says. "Have you visited the stars too?"

"Yes," I say and smile. "For there a few times I have flown, not for the music of the dance hall, not just for the peace, but for the dedication of the stars, who move whether or not they can feel it, whether or not they are seen."

"And so?" says the master.

I wait, for I do not know what to say next. I had heard the words and climbed the waves of mountains and laughed as the peaks tumbled under my feet. So, finally, I say, "Because no matter how many mountains I climb, no matter how many times I dance in the Coral Hall, I find myself in a world with carpets and floorboards that are nailed down, and that cannot tumble with the gods' laughter; I find myself here. I find myself having to remember the Coral Hall, instead of living in it."

The master smiles here, in an effort to contain his chuckle.

"The Coral Hall is not a place for one to live."

I wait.

"It is a place in which the living learn how to live, and it is nourished by our sincere desire to do so. It is a place in which the essence of how life can be lived is cultivated, but one cannot live there. Not one who intends to return back home, to other places."

I continue, "I do not know how to reconcile the difference between this world and that. But I know that exists. I have danced there! Why isn't that enough for me?"

"It is one thing," the master says, "to visit Egypt, by oneself, while one is sitting in Virginia. It is one thing to feel the texture of the mat on which one meditated 2000 years ago. This is exciting! It is like a new mountain to climb, but then we return to basecamp, we return home. We exit the the Great Coral Hall and find, all of a sudden, that it did not contain the whole world: it could not contain the whole world for now one is outside of it. The bells ring and the gongs are sounded. We are called by those here, now and not there, then. Here, at home, leaves seem to fall with no meaning. The wind blows, but we do not know what it says. The floors and carpets are nailed down here. The dragonflies mate in front of us, but we have to pee, or cook dinner, and so we do not see the great rainbows the energy of their union streaks across our lawns. The dance, here, has too many intermissions—intermissions between what people know, perceive, believe, feel, and understand. The music comes in fits and starts. This world is made up of disconnects between connections, not of the connections between disconnects. And so, my good student, you practice connection! You can transcend here and there, now and then! That is good! That is what you set out to learn! And now you also know, like those of us who continue our searching, that the more your soul transcends those separations, the more you come to understand the connectedness of everything, the more pronounced the distinctions between here and there and now and then might become to you. It is an odd consequence of the work you do.

"A person comfortable in time feels no such thing; a person who lives an ordinary life and does not seek to refine his soul, has no need to question where, when or what he is. He does not contrast what he sees, hears, or feels, with what is. But you, you have no such luxury. Now you contrast not part with part, as such a comfortable person would, but rather Whole with parts. And that, my dear, can seem to be a painful, insurmountable divide. But it is just a new mountain, a new gorge. Bigger than any you have experienced so far."

The master smiles at me. "You 'go away' to experience the unity of then and now and of there and here. You go from here, from the 'parts,' the fragments, the world of separation, to the 'whole.' You can fly adeptly back and forth now, like a bird to and from her nest."

"And the consequence of that is that I now feel how wide the gorge is between my nest and the world?" I ask. "What should I do?"

All he says is, "You want to experience the Great Hall, you want to dance with the stars, you want to feel the breeze as the wizards' cloaks flap in windless flight between the polestar and the star Vega? It is one thing to go out of oneself to experience creation and the universe; it is quite another to find the universe, to find here and now and there and then inside of you. You want to come home to the home of the universe without feeling afraid, then you must become the temple, the home, yourself."

"How?" I ask, quite sincerely.

The master laughs and says, "You will have to create where! And of course, when!"

I do not ask him if I will find the one I left battling waves of pain on the dock—the one I am always leaving, the one who makes me whole when I live in the world of fragments, the one I miss when I can feel the whole of the universe. But I know, in myself, that this is my question.

"How," I ask, knowing better, "do I do that?"

"You are already partway there," the master says. "When you are still, be like a mountain; when you move, be like water; when you sit, be like water; when you move, be like a mountain. When you do this, the mountains will multiply and the waters will flow eternally. As the mountains become so many and so still, they will create a river bed between them into which the waters will flow. Follow that river."

And so I sat. I put the Great Coral Hall in my mind and I watched as Wang Li danced with my mother, and my children from another life played with who they were to become as adults: the princess with the seamstress and the swordsman with the butcher and the mute with the inventor. The witch brewed tea for the sorcerer and the Taoist monk made clay pots with the widow of the tribal king, who, rather gleefully, was learning to play the flute with a young man who would eventually become her father. The music, I found, played on and on, no matter where my attention was, as though I lived in a house adjacent to the hall, with a window always open to it.

As I became absorbed in my voyeurism, a heavy dark cloud drew in from the western sky. Under it, the sun rose from the earth, but the cloud palmed it down, forcing the light and the heat to circulate between the leaves of the trees and the moist soil until the heat radiated so intensely that my heart, despite my stillness, shook inside of me. There are so many I have loved. I have lived in the past and the future and in each life, there